Also by Janice Lynn

The Doctor's Secret Son
A Firefighter in Her Stocking
A Surgeon to Heal Her Heart
Heart Surgeon to Single Dad
Friend, Fling, Forever?
A Nurse to Tame the ER Doc
The Nurse's One Night to Forever
Weekend Fling with the Surgeon

Discover more at millsandboon.co.uk.

REUNITED WITH THE HEART SURGEON

JANICE LYNN

MILLS & BOON

Published in Great Britain 2021
by Mills & Boon, an imprint of HarperCollins*Publishers* Ltd,
1 London Bridge Street, London, SE1 9GF

www.harpercollins.co.uk

HarperCollins*Publishers*
1st Floor, Watermarque Building,
Ringsend Road, Dublin 4, Ireland

Reunited with the Heart Surgeon © 2021 Janice Lynn

ISBN: 978-0-263-29216-9

05/21

MIX
Paper from
responsible sources
FSC™ C007454

Printed and bound in Great Britain
by CPI Group (UK) Ltd, Croydon, CR0 4YY

This book is dedicated to
medical professionals around the world.
Thank you for all you do.

PROLOGUE

NURSE NATALIE GIFFORD unlocked Dr. Will Forrest's door and let herself into the luxurious New York City penthouse. She'd never known money had a scent, but the condominium they'd shared the past six months reeked of it. Money. Wealth. Extravagance. The finest of everything.

Just like Will.

But not her. How had she ever thought a girl who'd grown up in a poor North Jersey neighborhood could fit into his life? That they could be a couple and function as equals in their relationship? If nothing else, her birthday party had proved to her that she'd just been fooling herself.

"Rough night?"

Startled, Natalie jumped. She'd expected Will to have left to make early-morning hospital rounds and she hadn't noticed where he stood by a row of windows overlooking Central Park.

As usual, he'd dressed his six-foot frame impeccably, wearing dark gray pants and a crisp white shirt with the top couple of buttons undone. Perhaps it was because he had grown up as the only child of one of America's wealthiest blue-blooded families that he had such an air of power and allure. Or it could be his rich dark brown hair and vivid green Harroway eyes which graced the most handsome face she'd ever looked upon that made him so appealing. Even after spending a tearful night at Callie's, asking herself why she'd had to fall for someone so beyond her world, seeing him made her pulse pound so fast her breath could hardly keep up.

That's why she'd fallen for him. Despite their many differences, her silly heart had led her to believe they could have a happy-ever-after. That dreams really did come true, and although not quite a Cinderella story, she could have the fairy tale with a real-life Prince Charming.

Despite his silverspoon upbringing, Will worked hard, genuinely cared about others and had completely wowed her when they'd met. Watching the kindness and compassion he showed while interacting with others had stolen her heart from the beginning and still gave her aww moments.

Watching Will stirred her no matter what he was doing. Quite simply, the man took her breath away.

He'd yet to turn toward her, but didn't question that it was her. The building's doorman had probably called to let him know she was on her way up before she'd even stepped foot into the elevator. Usually friendly, the doorman had given her messy bun, the ill-fitting jeans borrowed from her best friend, sandals, T-shirt, and the paper bag containing her party dress and heels a disapproving shake of his head. Yes, she had stayed out all night, but not because she'd been up to no good. She'd been nursing a broken heart. How horrible that her surprise twenty-fifth birthday party had ended with her crying on her best friend's sofa.

"You might say that," she admitted, pushing a stray auburn hair behind her ear as she stared at his stiff back. Did he regret their fight as much as she did? Was he ready to admit that his mother had intentionally used

Natalie's birthday party to drive home the differences in their socioeconomic backgrounds? Not that Natalie needed any help in recognizing the stark contrast. These days, she felt it more often than not. To put the icing on the cake, Rebecca Harroway Forrest had invited Will's "perfect for him" ex-girlfriend and kept throwing them together. When Will had given in to his mother's urging and danced with the woman, Natalie had had enough.

"How about you?" she quipped. "Rough night or did your mother send Stella over to comfort you?" She wouldn't have put it past Rebecca.

What had Natalie ever done other than love Will? But Rebecca's issues with her had nothing to do with how Natalie felt about Will and everything to do with the fact Natalie wasn't good enough for her precious son. Natalie didn't have the right pedigree or back account.

Will turned and the coolness in his eyes just about undid Natalie. She knew he was mad that she'd left her party without telling him. He'd made that clear during their brief phone exchange which she'd ended by hanging up on him. But she'd been mad, too. Livid. How dare he be so blind to Rebecca's meddling in their relationship, so tolerant of how she took every opportunity to let Natalie know she wasn't a welcome part of Will's life or their upper-crust family?

"Then you agree I was wronged and needed comforting?" His tone matched his gaze. She couldn't recall having ever seen that particular hue to his eyes before. Who knew green could look so cold?

"Not at all," she corrected. He'd been the one dancing with Stella Von Bosche. Yes, it had only been after Rebecca's urging, but *he should have said no.* "It was my night that was ruined."

His gaze narrowed. "Was something at your birthday party not up to your expectations?"

"A lot. For example, I expected my family and real friends there." She didn't attempt to hide her anger at the poor choices he'd made. For such a brilliant man, when it came to his family, he could be so clueless. "Not a bunch of strangers invited to purposely make me feel as if I didn't belong. And, you dancing with your ex-girlfriend absolutely wasn't something I expected."

Guilt flashed across his face, momentarily replacing the ice.

"If I'd realized it would bother you, I wouldn't have danced with Stella," he admitted.

Relief rushed through Natalie. His admission was a start in the right direction to soothing the unease she'd been experiencing more and more over the past few weeks. They never fought. Her gut twisted that they were now. Natalie's nature was to keep the peace, even to her own detriment. But not this time.

"You should have talked to me, not left without a word."

He wasn't wrong. She should have talked with him. At the time logic had been beaten down by her own emotions, and her self-doubts worsened by Rebecca's cooing over how wonderful it was that Stella was back in her son's life, how much they had in common and how no couple had ever been more perfect for each other. Natalie had had to leave. Either that or she'd have done something she would have regretted—like tell Rebecca what she thought of her.

"Do you know how I felt when I realized you were gone?" Raw emotion harshened Will's words. "That I had to make excuses at your own party for why you were no longer there?"

Nausea churned the few bites of breakfast she'd forced down at Callie's insistence. The entire night had been such a mess.

"I dare say you didn't feel nearly as upset as I did that leaving appealed more than staying at my birthday celebration. Then again, that party wasn't about me."

"If you'd stuck around, you'd have realized it was." Any semblance of calm was gone as he stepped away from the window. "I wanted to spend my night with you, and you left. *You left me.*"

His reactive, accusatory words both hurt and soothed her inner ache, but not enough to sway her sharp, defensive reply.

"You were barely with me when I was at the party." She lifted her chin, daring him to say otherwise.

"My father is up for reelection for his Senate seat. Spending a few minutes talking with his supporters shouldn't have been a problem." His brow arched. "Mother said you didn't appreciate—"

"That she invited your ex-girlfriend? That she planned my birthday party that you said was a surprise from you?" Natalie's anger surged. "Or that while I was listening to her go on and on about how perfect you and Stella were together and she just knew wedding bells were in your future, you were on the dance floor with said ex-girlfriend hanging all over you?"

"Natalie—"

"You seriously think I'm wrong to be upset?" she interrupted, gripping the sack she held tighter and crinkling the paper as her hand fisted. Part of her wanted to whack him with the bag to knock some sense into him.

Stopping to stand just in front of her, Will's gaze narrowed. "Stella's family are longtime friends of my family and she's Mother's goddaughter. I'll be cordial to her for that reason, if no other. Have I ever given you reason not to trust me, Natalie?"

He hadn't. That is, until she'd seen him laughing with Stella and felt the sharpest stab of pain she'd ever known, and all her doubts about their compatibility had exploded within her. After seeing him with Stella and Rebecca's words ringing in her ear, she'd felt so emotionally defeated she'd begged her only actual friends present, Callie and Brent, to get her out of the pretentious party.

"I don't appreciate not being trusted," he continued.

She jutted her chin upward. "I don't appreciate that your ex-girlfriend was at my birthday party."

"My mother—"

"Don't get me started about what I don't appreciate where that woman is concerned," she huffed, glaring at him.

Warning flashed in Will's eyes. "Stop right there, Natalie. You're treading on thin ice."

No doubt. Which was why she'd let Rebecca get away with her jabs time and again. Because Will would defend his mother to his dying breath. Why was Natalie bothering? They were so close that Will couldn't imagine his mother as anything other than Saint Rebecca. If Natalie told him everything the woman said and did, he wouldn't believe that Rebecca continually insinuated he was just passing the time until Stella returned.

And now, much to Rebecca's joy, Stella was back.

Natalie's stomach lurched. Her belly had been on edge the past few weeks as she'd felt Will's distraction, knowing he was keeping something from her and had grown withdrawn. Had Stella's return triggered the change in him, or had he just grown bored with Natalie?

The writing was on the wall. She could cut her losses or she could continue to live on edge, waiting to be tossed aside when Rebecca succeeded in driving a wedge so deep between them that they couldn't recover. Was that what the night before had been about? His mother smiling so happily as she'd surprised him with Stella's appearance?

No doubt anyone who'd looked their way would have thought Natalie and Rebecca were having a pleasant conversation as Rebecca smiled at the dancing couple while verbally inserting a knife into Natalie's heart and twisting it. For all Rebecca's gouging at her happiness, Natalie blamed Will as much, if not more, than she blamed his mother.

"Fine. I'm on thin ice, but guess what?" she spat back, months of biting her tongue unleashing. "So are you for being blind to the way your mother treats me. Thin, *cracked* ice."

"You're wrong," he defended, his brows furrowing. "Mother tries to reach out to you, but you're so biased you don't see that you push her away. That you let your insecurities about your background be a barrier to your relationship with her."

"Seriously?" Natalie rolled her eyes. "Is that what she tells you?"

"She asked to help me with your party because she wanted to do something special for you, to introduce you to our friends, and welcome you to the fold to let you know you're welcome."

"Of course she did." Natalie snorted. "And lucky for her that Stella came home to make the night even more welcoming."

Hands trembling, she turned to go. She really had had enough. If he'd loved her, she'd have been invincible to anything Rebecca tossed her way and would stay forever, but Will had never said he loved her. The one time she'd braved saying those three words out loud to him, he'd feigned being asleep. She should have known right then that they weren't meant to be.

Maybe she had, because wasn't that around the time she'd started feeling him pull away from her? Becoming more and more distant the weeks that followed?

She'd been such a fool. Love really was blind.

"Natalie!" Her name came out a bit ragged as he reached for her arm, stopping her from leaving. "You're behaving childishly."

Probably. The tears in her eyes certainly made her feel less adultlike.

"I can't believe you've allowed your bias about my mother to ruin your birthday party and lead us to spend a night apart." He sounded incredulous as he gently turned her to face him. "Nor can I believe we're fighting over my mother and Stella when there's no need."

Battling her tears, Natalie's heart thundered against her ribcage as he traced his finger over her cheek. Every nerve ending within her sparked to life like a Fourth of July show finale. Lord help her. It was no wonder she was putty in the man's talented hands. He touched her and she turned to mush. Only, she didn't want to be mush.

Not anymore. She wanted...

"Surely you know you have nothing to worry about where any woman is concerned?" he continued, his touch gentle as he cradled her face, forcing her to look up at him. He looked sincere, looked upset that they were at odds. Good. It upset her, too.

"How do I know that, Will?" she pressed even as tingles of awareness shot over her body just as they always did when he touched her. One little touch and she instantly wanted to kiss him until they were both breathless. Their chemistry was intense and had been from the moment they'd first met at the hospital when she'd dropped off lunch and a drink for Callie.

Will studied her, seeming surprised by her continued antagonism. "Because I want you."

Want. She needed more than want. Their explosive attraction was what had gotten her into this mess. One sexy I-want-you smile and conservative, play-it-safe, gonna-have-a-better-life-than-my-parents Natalie had been his for the taking. To be fair, all she'd had to do was give him a flirty look and he'd been hers for the taking, too. That Will had been so smitten had stunned her. When the good-natured cardiac surgeon, who also happened to be the only son of Senator William Forrest Sr. and business icon Rebecca Harroway Forrest, could have anyone, why Natalie?

Maybe that's why it was so easy for Rebecca's barbs to dig in.

Most days Natalie barely believed one of the city's most eligible bachelors wanted ordinary her.

"I'm tired of doubting myself, feeling as if I don't belong here, in your apartment, and in your life. I'm not willing to live like this, questioning myself all the time, questioning us, anymore. I deserve better."

"Questioning us?" He frowned. "I'm sorry you misunderstood about Stella, but if you'd stayed, you and I would have had an amazing night celebrating your birthday rather than a miserable one."

Natalie's insides shook. She might have misunderstood his dance with Stella, but there was nothing to misunderstand about what Rebecca had bluntly said. Nor the fact that Will refused to acknowledge that his mother had never approved of their relationship.

"I was miserable long before your dance with Stella," she admitted, realizing it was true and wondering how a person who made her so happy could also leave her feeling so unsure of herself. "It just took seeing you with her for me to admit to myself that I'd had enough."

To say he looked stunned was an understatement, and Natalie just stared as he asked, "You were miserable with me?"

Natalie put her hands on her hips as anger, frustration and so many emotions batted for pole position within her. Disgusted with herself, she flipped her hair back and spoke with more bravado than she actually felt.

"In case your memory is foggy, I wasn't with you," she pointed out, refusing to back down as all the things she'd been holding in poured from her. "I haven't been with you in weeks. Longer. You've been so busy and distracted that, other than at the hospital or at the Cancer Society for Children committee meetings, we've barely seen each other. You come home tired and distracted and won't talk to me about what's bothering you, even though I know something is. I feel the change in you and want to help and yet, you shut me out. Do you think I'm incapable of understanding? Or that I haven't felt the changes in our relationship? You and me—" she gestured to his chest, then her own "—we don't fit. I thought we did, but I was wrong."

The words gushed from her and, deep down, maybe she'd always known they were true. Maybe that's why she hadn't interrupted his dance or rebutted Rebecca's barbs, but had retreated to lick her wounds. Because part of her had always acknowledged Will would never be hers long term.

His face losing color, he took a step back. When his mouth opened, likely to remind her just how well they did fit together physically, she continued.

"At least, not outside the bedroom, we don't." Because

there was no denying how perfectly their bodies melded. Maybe that's all it had ever been, phenomenal sexual attraction and she'd been too naive to see the truth. "I thought we did—" oh, how she'd believed that "—but your mother was right and I was only fooling myself that we ever could. Whatever was between us is over. I'm done with trying to fit into your world and pretending that I ever could."

The skin on his face pulled tight, his cheeks flushing to an angry red.

Before he could tell her to get out, she said, "I'll pack a bag to take to Callie's and be back for the rest of my things."

Tell me not to go. Tell me you want me to stay. Tell me your mother will eventually approve of me despite my lack of pedigree and hefty bank account and that someday we can be a family. Tell me you love me.

He said none of those things.

What did she say to the man she loved when she didn't want to go, but when even on the verge of goodbye, he couldn't find words to convince her to stay?

Natalie sighed as she battled with the surrealness of what was happening. She was leaving Will. He was letting her go. They were ending. How could her fairy-tale romance have turned into a nightmare heartache?

"I'll have your other things delivered to Callie's later today."

"Okay," she choked out. "Thank you."

Heart breaking, she headed to the door.

"Natalie?"

Thank you, God.

She turned back, hoping he was going to tell her not to leave, that he'd make his mother understand how important she was, that he couldn't imagine his life without her, and then she'd run into his arms, they'd kiss and figure this out. They couldn't be ending.

They just couldn't.

Her gaze connected to his. His usual polished persona faltered and she got a brief glimpse that he wasn't as calm about her leaving as he'd appeared, but his next words shattered that illusion.

"Goodbye, Natalie. Have a nice life."

CHAPTER ONE

"If possible, I need you to swap my patient assignments," Natalie pleaded with the Cardiovascular Intensive Care Unit's nurse manager. "As in immediately, please. I can't work as Will's nurse."

Early that morning when she'd agreed to cover for another nurse who'd unexpectedly called in sick, she'd never imagined she'd be assigned Will's patients or she'd have refused to come in on her day off. Yes, she'd known it possible she'd see him, but thought she could mostly avoid him by staying busy in a patient room. Not that they traveled in the same circles, but having lived with him for six months, she knew his routine and the places he frequented.

Knew and had avoided them for the past month.

She'd not heard a peep from him since she'd walked out of his apartment on the morning after her birthday party. He'd had a moving company bring her boxed-up belongings that were, with a few unpacked exceptions, now stacked in the corner of Callie and Brent's spare bedroom, awaiting her decision on what she planned to do next. Her friends had set up a cot in the room they'd been using as an office, telling her to stay, and that they appreciated the rent money she'd insisted they take. She tried to make sure they had plenty of private time, but she knew it couldn't be any fun for the newlyweds to have her crashing in their space. She'd been volunteering a lot at the Cancer Society for Children to work on the gala and anything else Katrina had for her to do. She'd also signed on to work as many extra shifts as the hospital would let her. She'd been staying busy so she didn't have time to dwell on Will.

She'd like to say it was working, but unfortunately, she wasn't sure that level of busy existed.

"You have a problem working with Dr. Forrest?" the nurse manager asked, barely looking up from initialing papers on her desk.

Natalie stared at the older, stern woman. She'd seen her around the hospital a few times and always had a healthy respect for Callie's boss. Her bestie both admired and feared no-nonsense Gretchen and Natalie felt the same.

"I'd prefer not to work with him." Oh, how the tides had turned. Once upon a time she'd thought about putting in for a transfer to CVICU just so she could spend more time with Will. Thank goodness she'd decided against doing so or she'd be stuck seeing him over and over.

"Do you feel you can't professionally perform your job duties, Miss Gifford?"

Now, there was a loaded question. If she said she could, then there was no need of a patient assignment change. If she said she couldn't, then it made her look incompetent.

Staring the woman in the eyes, Natalie chose her words carefully. "I would have much higher job satisfaction if I wasn't Will—er... Dr. Forrest's nurse today or at any point in the future that I agree to fill in at the CVICU."

To put it mildly.

"You expect me to completely shuffle the schedule because of your personal relationship with Dr. Forrest?"

"Past personal relationship," Natalie clarified, her face heating. "And, yes, I would be appreciative if I didn't have to work directly with him." Why was the woman giving her a hard time? After all, she'd agreed to come in to help and in some ways was doing the lady a favor by ensuring the floor had enough nursing staff. "Surely, you understand my request given the circumstances?"

The thought of seeing Will made her head spin and her heart hurt. How was she supposed to focus on her patients when he was near and no longer hers? When there would be no more special smiles or winks when their eyes met? When he wouldn't go out of his way to make her laugh or to brush his hand against hers or whisper sweet nothings in her ear? Or…or refuse to believe his mother was out to destroy their relationship? Refuse to treat Natalie as his equal and someone he was proud to have at his side when attending his father's political fundraising events or the Harroway Foundation business dinners he'd gone to without her?

"Can you professionally perform your job duties?" the nurse manager repeated, her tone brooking no argument and suggesting that Natalie had best answer correctly.

It appeared she was going to have to see him. Her relationship with Will had already cost her heart and countless hours of sleep. She wouldn't allow it to affect a job she'd always loved.

"Yes."

"Then go do them."

Frustrated, Natalie reentered the CVICU unit, and signed in to her patient's chart, trying to focus on the orders even though her mind raced. Before the day was over, she'd see Will, have to interact with him, have to pretend they'd never meant anything to each other. Was she really that good an actress?

Was it possible that maybe her heart had grown immune to his many charms in the weeks since she'd last seen him?

Spotting her, Callie joined her at the nurses' station. Correctly reading her expression, her friend asked, "She wouldn't change your assignments?"

The words on the screen blurring, Natalie sighed. "She wouldn't even consider it. It's my own fault. I should have put that stipulation in when I agreed to cover for Connie this morning. I just never thought, well, you know."

"Oh, Nat. I'm glad you're here, getting to work with me just like back in nursing school, but I'm sorry she wouldn't swap your patient assignments." Callie made a face, then brightened. "Problem solved. I'll take care of your patients and you take care of mine. Both of my patients are admitted to Dr. Kumar. No big deal on the swap."

No big deal prior to her conversation with her nurse manager, perhaps.

Natalie shook her head. "Thank you, but after how adamant she was about her schedule not being disrupted I have a feeling I'd be fired if we swapped, or at the minimum, written up. Which would be bad enough on my end, but I'd never forgive myself if you got in trouble, too."

Callie's eyes widened. "You think? Why would they do that? Why should they give a flying flip how our patients are divvied up so long as we provide excellent care to them all?"

"Who knows? Maybe it's because a wealthy doctor whose family pours a ton of charity money into the hospital is involved." Natalie shrugged. "There's a wing named after his great-grandfather. They'd think nothing of letting me go if there's the slightest tension."

Callie frowned. "Why would they care if you're assigned to his patients or not? Looks like they'd want to make things easier by avoiding potential conflict."

So one would think. Natalie sure hadn't expected to get a no when she'd asked to swap."Who knows? Maybe Will will take one look at me being on the unit and let it be known that he doesn't want me assigned to his patients today, and that'll be that."

No way would the nurse manager deny *his* request. Not when his family was so generous to the hospital.

While working in the CVICU, she wouldn't be able to avoid seeing him, but if she wasn't assigned to his patients, it would help. No doubt he'd be doing his best to avoid her, as well. Maybe things wouldn't be as bad as she feared. Maybe she'd be over him and the mere sight of him wouldn't send her heart into palpitations.

"I'm being paranoid." Wanting to bang her head against the fuzzy computer screen, Natalie sighed. "Don't listen to me. I'm just aggravated that I'm being forced to work with him when the last thing I want is to lay eyes on Will Forrest ever again."

"I'll keep that in mind."

Natalie and Callie spun at the sharp words.

"Will!" Natalie gasped, her heart slamming against her ribcage as her gaze ate up the sight of him. So much for hoping a month had left her immune to him. If anything, all time had done was make her that much more aware of how every fiber of her being yearned for him.

His deep green eyes regarded her, his expression terse, reminiscent of the coolness with which he'd looked at her that last morning at his apartment. Time didn't seem to have made his heart grow fonder, because any fool could see that he wasn't happy she was there, in the CVICU, on his turf. How long had he been standing there? Had he heard her talking about his mother? Ugh. She should have known better. She did know better.

"I mean, Dr. Forrest," she corrected, not willing to let him be the one to tell her to address him more formally as she no longer had the right to call him by his first name.

All she had left was her dignity and she wouldn't let him take that, too. His expression didn't change, other than his eyes darkening further before turning to address Callie.

"Which nurse is assigned to Mattie Johnson?"

"Natalie, but I'll be happy to round with you," Callie offered despite their previous conversation about the nurse manager refusing to switch patient assignments. No doubt her friend was trying to save her.

His lips tightened. "Is there a reason why Natalie can't provide care for her patients?"

"No reason," Natalie jumped in before Callie felt further obligated to rescue her from this awkward situation. How many times had she wondered what it would be like to see Will again? Now she knew.

"Let me get logged out of this chart, and I'll be right with you," she said to buy herself a few seconds to collect her wits. After not seeing him for a month, she was face-to-face with the man she'd once thought she'd spend the rest of her life with. How could she have been so naive? Men like him didn't marry social nobodies like her.

Now, at least for the day, they'd be coworkers. Her nurse to his doctor because both of her patients belonged to Will.

"By all means take your time." His sarcasm wasn't lost on her. "It's not as if our patients in CVICU are critical."

Will's judgmental tone irked. How dare he stare down

his snooty nose at her as if she'd done something wrong in saying she was going to log out of the chart she was in. She hadn't, and he knew good and well that she couldn't walk away from a computer that had a logged-in patient on the screen.

All she'd ever wanted to be was a registered nurse and she strove to be a good one. Today, taking care of his patients, was no exception. Other than for the remainder of her shift she'd be pretending that he hadn't broken her heart.

Darn him for making her question herself. For making her pulse pound, for making her nerves jittery, and shattering her dreams of a happy-ever-after. Just…darn him.

Clicking to log out on the chart her fuzzy brain had failed to decipher anyway, Natalie narrowed her gaze in feigned disgust—or maybe it was real. She'd given him her heart. Shouldn't he have had her back? Even when it came to his mother? Regardless, she glared long enough she hoped he got the point. She didn't plan to pine away for him—or, at least, not let him know she was.

She'd do her best to concentrate on her patients. It was only for a day. She could do this.

Mattie Johnson was a sixty-year-old African American woman who'd gone to the emergency room via ambulance with chest pain and ended up admitted with a "widow-maker" early that morning. Thank goodness the woman hadn't delayed in activating the emergency system or she likely would have died from the significant blockage of the main artery supplying her heart with oxygenated blood. Will had just arrived at the hospital to prep for a routine procedure, which had gotten pushed back while he stented the woman's left anterior descending artery, restoring oxygenated blood flow to her heart and saving her life. After she was stable enough, she'd been transferred to the CVICU, which had occurred just prior to shift change.

And she'd been assigned to Natalie.

Will's gaze narrowed slightly at her scowl, then without another word, he walked away, leaving Natalie and Callie to watch him leave.

Natalie's heart squeezed and she fought to keep from saying his name to call him back. She wouldn't.

What would it matter if she did? He'd been hers and she'd chosen to leave, a little voice reminded. Only, he hadn't been hers. Not really. If he had, he still would be. She'd decided in the past few weeks that his mother had been right. He'd been Stella's all along and Natalie had just been a fun way to pass the time until his true love came home. She had been convenient, and the sex had been great, so why not? Otherwise, he'd have come after her, right? Or he would have at least called or texted or reached out in some way to let her know that he was sorry, that he missed her, that absence really had made his heart grow fonder.

"You okay?"

Not meeting Callie's eyes, Natalie nodded. She needed to do her job and to not let her personal life seep into her workday. She couldn't afford to lose her job.

"I know seeing him wasn't easy."

Ha. That was the understatement of the year. Who wanted to see their superhot cardiac surgeon gazillionaire ex-boyfriend after the breakup? After the he's-the-one-I'm-going-to-marry euphoria had morphed into heartbreak and tears? Why couldn't his hold over her heart have loosened over the weeks apart?

"It'll get easier."

Natalie couldn't fathom how. She'd not been willing to live the rest of her life as things had been, with his not valuing her role in his life and his refusing to see the truth about his mother. But maybe she hadn't thought out the whole living-without-Will bit as thoroughly as she should have.

Still, if she had to have Will as an ex, then at least she could hold her head high knowing she'd been the one to walk away rather than waiting for him to kick her to the curb. Yes, everyone probably thought her crazy, but at least she could cling to that small tidbit as she was bombarded with sympathy from her well-meaning coworkers.

"You're right. Things will get better." She smiled at Callie and thanked God she had such a great best friend. She needed to keep her thoughts trained on the good in life. A month had passed. She'd survived. She had this. "I'm going to check on Mrs. Johnson. Thanks for everything, Cal."

Right before Natalie had spoken with the nurse manager, Mrs. Johnson's readings had essentially been the same as the night nurse had reported at shift change.

Will must have gone to a different patient room since Mrs. Johnson was still alone in her room. At first glance Natalie knew something had changed during the short time lapse between checks. She listened to the woman's chest and didn't like the raspy breath sounds she heard. Nor that the woman's oxygen saturation level had dropped some despite her being on oxygen via a nasal cannula. Not enough that her monitor alarm had sounded, but a few percentage points.

"Mrs. Johnson?" she said, hoping the woman responded and her vitals improved with some deep breathing exercises. Perhaps she was just in a deep sleep and that's why her vitals had declined.

Mrs. Johnson opened her eyes, but never fully focused

on Natalie before closing them again. She'd been sleeping when Natalie had been in the room earlier, too.

"Mrs. Johnson, I need you to take a few deep breaths for me." Some big ones in the hope it would help clear her noisy chest and increase her oxygen saturation.

The woman's eyelids flickered, but that was the only response to Natalie's request.

"Mrs. Johnson, it's time to wake up. You need to use your incentive spirometer." She attempted to rouse her patient with a gentle shake of her shoulder, again to no avail. So much for gently trying to wake the woman. Natalie clenched her fist and rubbed her knuckles across the woman's chest in a sternal rub meant to elicit a pain response. She got a flinch from the lethargic woman, but nothing more.

She glanced at the monitor screens. Nothing was so out of line that she should be alarmed, but something more was going on. Sometimes it happened that a patient just needed rest and didn't wake much post-surgery, especially one as critical as Mrs. Johnson's early morning procedure. But Natalie didn't like the fact that she couldn't get the woman to wake.

Was Will still with his other patients? Whether she wanted to interact with him or not, she was going to have to call him to the room.

Will paused outside Mattie Johnson's room when he realized Natalie was with his patient. Since she'd not been at the nurses' station, he'd known he'd likely see Natalie in Mattie's room.

Like a glutton for punishment, he'd practically ordered her there.

To check his patient, he assured himself. Because he'd operated on Mattie and was making rounds. Of course he'd check the woman prior to leaving the CVICU and would want to discuss how she was doing and her care with her nurse. It's what he did.

His reasons didn't have anything to do with seeing Natalie and how his gaze had immediately latched onto her when he'd entered the CVICU. Thanks to an early-morning call saying Natalie was covering in the unit, he'd known she'd be there. Was it wrong that when a friend in human resources had asked, he'd told them it was fine for her to care for his patients if that's how the assignments naturally fell? That she was an excellent nurse, and he didn't want his patients deprived of her nursing skills? Probably. He'd not wanted to risk the hospital dinging Natalie's career in any way if he'd said he'd rather her not be on the unit. Plus, he had wanted the best for his patients. Natalie was.

The best at a lot of things.

Part of him still couldn't wrap his brain around the past month. How he'd gone from feeling as if she completely adored him to—her words from earlier popped into his head—to her not wanting to see him at all.

How was that even possible?

He'd felt powerless when she'd walked out of their apartment with her suitcase. Completely gutted. Something he wasn't used to feeling and didn't know quite how to deal with. She'd left him. If she cared for him, how could she have done that over what he considered nothing more than a misunderstanding?

Knowing he was going to come face-to-face with her for the first time in a month had kept him hyperaware of every breath, every beat of his heart as he'd made his way to the unit. Would their eyes meet just as they had the first time he saw her and would his world shift again? Or had her abandoning their relationship killed his feelings for her?

How could she have just walked away without fighting for what they shared? If she'd loved him as she claimed, she wouldn't have left.

Yet, she had.

Which told him all he needed to know. Just as well that he'd choked up when she'd whispered those three words to him one night after they'd made love. After his failed relationship with Stella, and then with Natalie, Will didn't know what love was, but he had a lot of experience with what it wasn't.

Still, overhearing Natalie's conversation with Callie first thing had knocked him hard, again. Not only did she not regret leaving, but she didn't want to see him, period. That shouldn't matter. It didn't matter, right? She'd left. A month had passed. Of course, she didn't want to see him. Only a fool would have thought otherwise.

Will was no fool.

But when he'd heard she'd agreed to work on his floor, he'd wondered if maybe she wanted to see him, maybe she…never mind what he'd felt when he'd gotten that call. It didn't matter.

He'd been devoted to their relationship and she hadn't. Why had she gotten so upset? Because his overwhelmed mother had wanted to help with her party, and he'd been thrilled that even with as much as she had going on, she wanted to do that for Natalie? He'd hoped maybe for once Natalie would see that his mother wasn't the enemy? Or was she mad because he'd danced with Stella?

That Natalie had jumped to conclusions and walked away spoke volumes. She hadn't trusted him. That cut deep. He'd dealt with jealousy in the past, even with Stella. Relationships were doomed to fail when there was no trust, and to pretend otherwise was a waste of a couple's time.

Not that he'd given Natalie any reason not to trust him. Admittedly he had been distracted by his mother finding a lump in her breast and trying to keep it hush-hush when she went for testing, because she'd insisted no one know. Which included Natalie. Harroway Industries was in billion-dollar negotiations to buy out a tech company that held the patent on a revolutionary 3D-printed two-sided circuit board. His mother refused to risk anything— including her health—affecting the deal. Obtaining the patent was huge for Harroway's future growth and they'd been just one of many companies wooing the firm.

In his efforts to be there for his mother and lighten her load at the foundation, had Will been so preoccupied he'd missed seeing that Natalie had become disenchanted with their relationship, and was thus taken by surprise at her leaving when he should have seen it coming? Or had his concern over his mother's health crisis been the catalyst that had pushed Natalie away?

Where his mother was concerned, Natalie had never thought rationally, always assuming his mother didn't like her and wanted them apart. He'd talked to his mother about how Natalie felt, urging her to reach out, to make her feel more welcome. He'd been thrilled when she offered to help with Natalie's party. He'd wanted Natalie to learn to feel comfortable around his mother so she'd want to go with him to dinners and business functions. Instead, the party had been a disaster. Natalie had left upset. His mother's feelings had been hurt.

His mother had always been invincible. As if his breakup with Natalie wasn't enough, watching his mother struggle to keep up her public facade was tearing him to bits. Tough as nails, she insisted she could beat her cancer without the world being privy to her private hell. God, Will hoped so. He couldn't imagine the alternative. He'd wanted to share his fears with Natalie, to hold her tight and have her tell him it was going to be okay. But the one time he'd tried, she'd become so prickly at the mention of his mother, he'd held his worries inside, instead.

Seeing her at the hospital shouldn't have been a big deal, but it still left him unsettled. To the degree that he decided he'd finish with all his other patients prior to checking on Mattie in hopes of avoiding direct interaction with Natalie.

But she was still there.

He'd wait, come back later, at lunch maybe, and hopefully avoid bumping into Natalie again.

Just as he started to walk away without her having known he'd been outside the patient room he noted the rising concern in her movements as she shook Mattie's shoulder and insisted the woman wake up.

Something was wrong.

He rushed into the room. "What's going on?"

Natalie's only reaction to him was to briefly flick her gaze his way before returning her attention to her patient. "She doesn't want to wake. Her oxygen is dipping into the mid-eighties, and her lungs sound junky when they didn't earlier. I don't like what I'm seeing or hearing. I was just about to call you."

"Mattie?" He attempted to get a response from his patient. Her eyelids fluttered, but she never opened them. "Mrs. Johnson," he said more brusquely, shaking her shoulder as he did so. "Open your eyes and look at me."

One eye peeped open just enough for Will to know she was at least somewhat aware of what was happening around her.

"Mattie," he purposely repeated her name. "Are you hurting anywhere?"

His patient's hand moved a little, but she never pointed out any particular spot.

A machine dinged, sounding its alarm.

"Her oxygen saturation dropped to 83 percent," Natalie warned as she adjusted the woman's airway tubing, making sure flow was unimpeded.

Mattie had been breathing normally on her own earlier when Will had removed her intubation after her surgery. She'd looked good when he'd checked on her in recovery.

"Increase her liter per minute flow rate," Will ordered as he examined his patient. Her lungs were crackling. She was prophylactically anticoagulated, but had she thrown a clot? Or was she coming down with pneumonia or in fluid overload? Either could explain what they were hearing. "If that doesn't increase her saturation, then mask her. Also, let's get a CT scan on her chest."

Assuming they got her stable and he didn't have to put her back on a ventilator. As if Mrs. Johnson had read his mind and was preempting him, her blood oxygen saturation dropped further. Her heart rate sped up, then drastically dipped. Another warning alarm sounded.

"Mattie?" Natalie tried to stir her in hopes of rallying her vitals as she changed her nasal cannula over to a face mask in an attempt to increase the woman's blood oxygen concentration.

It didn't work and another alarm dinged, causing Will's gaze to go to the significantly decreased oxygen ratio.

"Do you want me to start bi-pap therapy to try to regulate her breathing?" Natalie asked.

Will nodded. Maybe it would be enough, and they wouldn't have to put her on a vent. Only, before Natalie could even get the woman hooked up to the respirator machine, her breathing worsened.

Mattie was spiraling into a complete crash right before their eyes.

He needed to put her back on the ventilator.

Without his saying a word, Natalie went into action, immediately changing course. They worked together seamlessly, Natalie knowing what to do without his ever having to ask. She'd always been great at anticipating his needs, filling them.

Once he had the tube inserted down Mattie's airway, his gaze cut to the monitor and he gave a sigh of relief. Her numbers had instantly improved. Taking his stethoscope, he listened over her lung fields, pleased at the air movement the ventilation machine was providing.

"Placement sounds good, but her chest CT will double-check it," he said, planning to enter in the order for the test, but Natalie was a step ahead and was already punching the order into Mattie's computerized chart.

Once Mattie's heart rate had calmed and her chest was rising and falling rhythmically from the machine breathing for her, Will checked her over one last time, assessing for any external clue of what was going on to cause her crash and finding nothing unexpected.

"Did she say anything prior to my coming into the room?"

Natalie shook her head. "She opened her eyes when I tried to wake her, the same as she attempted to do with you, but she never seemed aware of where she was or who I was."

Pulling off his gloves and tossing them into a waste bin, Will accidentally brushed up against Natalie. At the same moment he registered they were touching, she jumped back as if scalded, crossing the room to stand far away from him and Mattie's bed.

"Don't," he couldn't keep from saying, even though he immediately regretted having revealed how her reaction had gotten to him.

Natalie's gaze lifted at his ground-out word.

"Don't act as if my touch offends you," he elaborated, moving to stand near her so they could keep their voices down, and thinking for a moment that she was going to relent, apologize for her lack of faith in him and their relationship, and tell him she'd missed him. He'd swear that was what the emotions in her eyes were conveying, but rather than agreeing, she lowered her gaze to hide whatever shone there.

"Let's not have this conversation here, Will."

"Then where?" he demanded, wondering what it mattered at this point. They were over. He didn't want her back. So, what did any of this matter?

"I…" She hesitated, then keeping her gaze averted, asked, "Is there a need to have a conversation at all?"

His breathing halted. Thank God no monitors were attached to alert her to his body's response to the thought she no longer cared about him, that seeing him didn't affect her the way seeing her affected him.

"You tell me. You're the one who left." He hadn't meant to sound so accusing.

"You're right. I did." Her gaze narrowed and she tossed out an accusation of her own. One that stung Will to the core. "But you're the one who left me at home night after night. No wonder you encouraged me to take a more active role on the Children's Cancer Gala committee. That way I wouldn't be home to notice you never were."

"Of course I wanted you on the committee. I'm on it, too, remember?" He'd known she'd give the gala her all and do a great job for an important charity, ensuring its success. It was a cause he believed in and thought she had, too. That had been before he'd known of his mother's cancer diagnosis and how pulled into a dozen directions he'd be. As much as he'd hated to, he'd missed the last meeting. "You knew I was a cardiac surgeon when we got together. I'm going to get called into the hospital—"

"It's not the hospital calling that was the issue," she cut in, ungloved hands on her hips.

"My mother—"

"Was a big problem in our relationship," she interrupted again, keeping her voice at barely above a whisper. Although unconscious, neither of them wanted to risk Mattie being aware of their conversation in whatever realm her mind currently functioned.

"Be careful what you say," he warned, his jaw tightening. Natalie was so sweet and kind with everyone except the other woman who mattered most in his life. Why couldn't they have gotten along?

"Because we're talking about your mother and that's a big no-no topic?" she scoffed, her eyes glinting. "We should have talked about how she undermined our relationship from the moment she met me, months ago, and was appalled that you were dating a nobody. She must be over the moon that I'm gone."

Natalie's defiant tone startled him. She'd never talked this way. He'd thought she understood his role as an only child. He might have gone into medicine, but he still had family obligations to his late grandfather's company, to the charity foundation that had grown out of the corporation— the Harroway Foundation, that his mother ran—and to his parents. Ever since his mother's biopsy on the breast mass had come back as invasive carcinoma, she had needed him more than ever. Things would be simpler if Natalie knew the reason he'd been so tied up with his mother, but she should trust there was a good reason why he wasn't at home. Shouldn't she have had his back when times were tough without his having to ask her to?

Is there anything wrong with Natalie? his mother had questioned him as to why she'd left her birthday party.

Not that she's said. His mother had been genuinely worried Natalie hadn't liked her party. Not wanting to add to her stress, he'd merely responded that he and Natalie had realized their relationship wasn't working and gone their separate ways. His mother was dealing with enough, with her radiation treatments and hiding her illness, without worrying about the demise of his relationship or why Natalie didn't like her.

He didn't need to worry about it, either.

Too bad his body was still pro-Natalie. No woman had ever affected him the way she did. Still, he hadn't expected to feel so tightly wound at seeing her again. Crazy as it was, her eyes sparking fire, her chin high and her hands on her hips sent a surge of testosterone through his system. He shouldn't want her. Not under these circumstances. Not at all since she'd so easily turned her back on him. But his body reacted to Natalie like gasoline tossed on fire. It's how it had always been physically between them. Did she feel it, too? Did she see him and have a thousand regrets the way he did?

"Let's go somewhere after work and talk."

The light in her eyes flickered, dimming a little, indecision emanating from her.

"I can meet you here at the end of your shift and we'll get dinner," he offered, seeing the softening on her face and seizing the opening she was giving him, although he wasn't sure why. They'd been apart a month. Would saying he was sorry even matter at this point?

"I…are you sure you want to do that?"

Was he? Staring down into her eyes, seeing the indecision and wariness, he felt gutted. They'd been so close, and now…they weren't. That couldn't be right.

"We need peace between us, don't you think?"

She looked away, again. "Do we?"

"We work in the same hospital. Our paths will cross. It would make things easier if we didn't have animosity between us."

She sighed. "Okay. We'll go to dinner. Will, I—" Her lashes fluttered. But rather than finish her comment, she gazed beyond him and her cheeks pinkened. "Um, thank you, Dr. Forrest," she said in her most formal tone as she pulled away from him. "I've got that chest CT and labs entered into the system and will have Radiology and the lab call you directly with the results."

Face still flaming, she rushed from the room.

Frowning at the interruption, Will turned to see what had caught her eye. Her nurse manager stood outside the doorway. Disapproval shone in the woman's dark eyes.

Will gave her a curt nod, then went to document Mattie's incident. Part of him was disappointed they'd been interrupted before Natalie could finish her sentence. Even more, he was disappointed in himself, for his desire to follow her and ask.

His pulse pounded in anticipation of an evening spent with Natalie, even if it was only an hour or so spent talking about things he'd thought over and done with.

Would he and Natalie ever truly be over and done with?

CHAPTER TWO

ALL DAY NATALIE'S stomach had been a tight mess. All week, really. No wonder with her nerves on edge. Would Will come by at the end of her shift as he'd said prior to her spotting Gretchen and making a run for it? Why had she agreed to go to dinner with him? Not that she didn't know. He'd crooked that finger and she'd instantly wanted to say yes to anything he asked for, just like always.

Weak. Weak. Weak, she scolded herself. Had she learned nothing over the past month?

Why was she questioning whether he'd come by? Physically, he wanted her. She'd seen it in his eyes when he'd accidentally brushed against her. Emotionally, well, despite his lack of verbalizing those words she longed to hear him say, once upon a time, she'd believed he cared about her. Wasn't that why she'd been so willing to fall into his life? Because she'd believed that and hoped that eventually their worlds would meld together? She'd been so wrong.

The real question was whether she should go any-where with him or cancel completely so they didn't end up between his fancy high-count Egyptian cotton sheets.

What was she saying? She had fallen head over heels for him, but what woman privileged enough to be a part of his life hadn't? She wasn't happy with the way things had become between them, but hadn't her ultimate wish been for them to work things out? For them to find some happy medium where his mother was concerned? Where the disparities in their relationship could be overlooked so they were on equal ground with each other? If he was willing to make concessions, to see her point of view and make changes in how he handled their relationship, especially regarding his mother, wouldn't she want to hear what he had to say?

If nothing else, her birthday party had taught her how fragile their relationship really was and even more so, how fragile her confidence in his feelings toward her were.

Natalie had no option but to meet Will, but she was determined not to let the sexual sparks between them lull her brain.

She was going to have to be careful not to get distracted by him while at work, too. Her nurse manager had been watching her with hawklike eyes all day, as if waiting for some misstep so she could call her into the office for reprimanding.

"That must be one interesting chart you're documenting."

Natalie glanced up at her bestie's comment. "Nothing like a patient throwing a pulmonary embolism and a thrombosis in her left lower extremity gastrocnemius vein despite being anticoagulated to keep life from being boring."

"Better you than me." Callie gave a dramatic quiver. "Stable now, though?"

Natalie nodded. "Yes, Mrs. Johnson is stable. Will... I mean, Dr. Forrest..." She stopped, met Callie's eyes, then shrugged. "Never mind."

Her friend gave her an empathetic look. "I think it's a

good thing you're going to dinner tonight. You still have feelings for him." Ugh. Was she that obvious? "Talk and maybe you will get things patched up."

Natalie didn't fool herself that their issues could be patched up over a single dinner. She wasn't convinced their issues could be patched up period. Will was who he was. Dr. William Harroway Forrest, heir of Harroway Industries and cochair of the Harroway Foundation, a duty shared with his mother. He was a talented heart surgeon, generous with his time and money to so many. She imagined she'd only been privy to a fraction of the good Will did as it wasn't something he talked about, but Natalie knew enough to know he had a big heart. Natalie was who she was. Nurse Natalie Jane Gifford, a woman who had lived her twenty-five years leading a hardworking life to be proud of, for the most part, even if her accomplishments were simple compared to Will's world. She was a woman who deserved to be loved, cherished, proudly shown off and treated as having equal weight in the relationship. All women deserved that and shouldn't settle for less.

Why had she?

Because when she'd brought Callie's forgotten lunch to her and bumped into the most gorgeous man she'd ever met, he'd smiled at her in a way that had made her heart race and her body glad to be alive. While she had waited on Callie to come out of a patient room, they'd chatted a few minutes. Her breathless and him all teasing and sexy grins. When she'd handed over Callie's lunch and started to walk away, he'd surprised her by asking if she was busy that evening. Her heart had cleared its schedule indefinitely.

Only, she hadn't known who he was. When he'd introduced himself as Will Forrest, she hadn't known anything of his wealthy, blue-blooded background. If only he could have just been the man she'd met that day forever, without the trappings of being the Harroway heir encroaching on their happiness, or their backgrounds having ever been a big deal.

He'd kept saying their differences didn't matter, but he hadn't been the one thrown into a world he'd not been accustomed to and had felt overwhelmed by. The only times she'd even come close to his glitzy world had been when she'd accompanied her housekeeper mother to some of the upscale apartments she'd cleaned and those had been nothing compared to Will's world. A memory of a particular family's kids laughing at her ill-fitting hand-me-down clothes hit her. She'd barely been school-age but recalled the moment vividly.

Rebecca Harroway Forrest had looked at her with the same disregard as her mother's employers had and, standing in the grandeur of the Harroway penthouse, Natalie had reverted to that ridiculed poor little girl rather than the young woman she was proud to have become.

Looking back, meeting Rebecca had been the turning point in her relationship with Will. He'd gone from an exciting man she was falling in love with to being a part of an elite club she wasn't a member of, could never really belong to, but might be allowed to play so long as she didn't cause any problems and stayed in the background. She'd been so caught up in their whirlwind romance that she'd not even realized what she was doing as she strove to make their relationship easy for him at all costs.

Deep down she'd been waiting for him to realize he'd made a mistake in thinking he wanted to be with her, and she hadn't wanted to make the end happen sooner by causing resistance of any kind.

Just like with the rich kids she'd encountered through

her mother's housekeeping, she only got to play if she went along with everything they wanted. So, she had. As a child. And, once she'd met Rebecca, she'd fallen into those ingrained habits with Will without realizing what she'd done until he'd started becoming emotionally distant and distracted when they were together.

Their issues lay as much with herself as with Will. She should have addressed how she felt the moment she realized, talked with him about the way his mother made her feel. She shouldn't have let it reach the point of complete resentment and emotional breakdown it had at her birthday party when she'd looked around at the glamourous party, realized none of her family and real friends were there, and known that this wasn't the life she wanted.

Did she really want that? To have to constantly prove her worth to Will's high-society friends and family who seemed to only value bank accounts and social status and not what was on a person's inside?

She'd tried talking to him about his mother a few times, but he refused to see anything except what Rebecca wanted him to see. As entangled as her heart was with Will, nothing had changed. What purpose would it serve for them to go to dinner? She wouldn't go back to being a yes girl. Not even for Will.

Callie motioned to the hallway leading to the CVICU. "He's here, but don't look because his eyes are trained right on you and aren't budging as he heads this way."

Natalie's heart somersaulted. To Will's credit, he'd returned to the unit fifteen minutes before the end of her shift and not left her to awkwardly wait to see if he showed.

"Callie, Natalie," he greeted when he reached the nurses' station. Rather than linger, with a quick meeting of their eyes that acknowledged his main purpose for being there, he headed to Mattie Johnson's room.

Since Natalie had finished her charting and the night nurse taking her place hadn't shown yet for report, she went to check on her patients, saving Mrs. Johnson for last so that odds were higher that Will would have already left the CVICU room.

But he hadn't.

"Dr. Forrest," she acknowledged where he stood by Mattie's bed. "I thought I'd do one last check before giving report at shift change. Do you want me to come back later?"

His gaze colliding with hers, he shook his head. "There's no need for that, Natalie."

Heart pounding so loudly she worried the reverberations might alter Mattie's telemetry, Natalie checked her patient while her doctor watched her sleep.

Still on the ventilator and unconscious, Mattie's vitals were holding steady.

"She's been stable since you intubated her," Natalie said, although she wasn't telling him anything he wasn't well aware of. He'd kept close tabs on the woman all day.

Watching her examine Mattie, he nodded. "Thanks to your quick actions this morning in realizing something wasn't right she should be fine. We'll let her rest and watch her extra close over the next twenty-four hours."

Natalie's face heated at his praise. She'd done nothing more than what any nurse would have done.

"I got lucky that I was in here when she started crashing." Natalie kept her gaze trained on the rise and fall of Mattie's chest rather than look toward Will. Looking toward him, meeting those amazing eyes trained on her, tied her stomach into knots. "Anything in particular you want me to convey to her night nurse?"

"Just what you normally would, and the morning lab orders that I put into her chart earlier. I'd like them drawn and back by the time I round in the morning."

"I'll note it." Natalie finished assessing her patient, with Will at the bedside. When she was done, she hesitated. How could being near him feel so right where she wanted to be, and so awkward and nerve-racking and not okay at the same time?

Because when it was just the two of them, everything had felt perfect. Those moments of going for a walk in Central Park or sitting out on his balcony for hours just talking had melded her heart to him. A memory popped into her head of the time he packed a picnic and they spent an afternoon flying a kite of all things. How they'd laughed at their silliness, at how good it felt to be together.

Oh, how her heart ached at that loss.

She missed him. A month hadn't lessened how she yearned for his smile, his laughter, his simply telling her good morning. If they could have shut the world out forever, they'd have been just fine. But that wasn't reality. Nor would she have wanted it to be that way. Not really. If they had any chance of working things out, they had to accept who the other was. The good. The bad. The ugly. She had to keep her voice and get over her hesitancy, her self-doubts and her willingness to settle for anything less than being his partner in every sense of the word. And, then there was his mother. She wouldn't put up with her interfering in their relationship forever, either.

Although, if he'd loved her, she'd have waited indefinitely.

Glancing at her watch, she saw it was past time for the night nurse to have arrived. She needed to get back to give report.

"I'll wait here with Mattie," he said, reading her well. In many ways, he'd always read her well. She shouldn't have worked so hard hiding her insecurities. If she had let him see her struggles more, how unsure she felt in his world, would it have made a difference? If she'd stressed to him how his mother made her feel? Or would they just have ended sooner?

"When you're off the clock, let me know, and we'll head out," he told her, his gaze never leaving hers.

Natalie swallowed. Hard. Because so many memories of his waiting on her shift to end, of their leaving the hospital together, hand in hand, to go on some adventure around the city or just straight home for an adventure all their own.

"Yes. We'll go talk." She wanted to talk, wanted to hear what he had to say, couldn't not hear what he had to say, and maybe she'd say things she'd held in too long. Doing that would be good for her. Good for him to hear, too, because he needed to know what was in her heart. Still, what she didn't want was to get caught up in the same mind fog she experienced when he was near. She glanced toward their unconscious patient, then walked out into the hallway, not really surprised when he followed her.

She paused, took a deep breath. "Promise me something?"

His brow lifted.

"No touching," she said low enough that only he'd be able to hear. Not that anyone seemed to be paying them the slightest attention, but she didn't want to risk it.

He frowned. "What kind of promise is that?"

"The one I need you to make," she reiterated, knowing his agreeing was vital to her sticking to her goals. His touch held too much control over her willpower. "We're going to talk," she whispered, "not get distracted by sexual attraction. Please, promise me."

"No touching?" He regarded her a moment, then nodded. "If that's what you want, then no touching it is."

"Thank you."

He shrugged as if it were no big deal, then added, "Your loss, though."

Yeah, she was well aware of that. Unfortunately.

No touching. What had Natalie thought? That he was going to drag her back to his place for— He shook his head to clear it as he walked back over to Mattie Johnson's hospital bed.

Staring down at the unconscious woman, he wondered what she was thinking or if she was in a peaceful rest. The rise and fall of her chest was rhythmic, lulling one into a false sense of calm.

Will didn't feel calm.

He felt…torn. What was he doing asking Natalie to go to dinner with him? After all, he'd decided that with his mother's breast cancer his being single was probably for the best. Best for his mother. But for Will, despite the month apart, he longed to tell Natalie everything. On every subject other than his mother, she was the best listener. If he told her his mother might be dying, she'd understand why he'd been so distracted. Will had trusted Natalie completely, but his mother had reminded him of the fallout to the company if word got out of her illness and it affected their acquisition, and following that how many of their loyal employees and stockholders were in jeopardy. They couldn't risk the consequences if he was wrong about Natalie. He'd never thought he was, but he'd not anticipated Natalie leaving him, either.

Sighing, Will reached down, placed his hand over

Mattie's still one, saying a silent prayer for the woman's speedy recovery, then, "I'll be back in the morning. Have a good night's rest and wish me luck."

Wish him luck? Luck for what exactly? What was it he hoped to gain by taking Natalie to dinner?

To get his friend back because he missed her.

To get his girl back because he missed her.

To get his lover back because he missed her.

Will sucked in a deep breath and reminded himself that Natalie had walked away from him when he'd needed her. She'd judged him wrongly at her birthday party, condemning him without cause, and let her own insecurities poison their relationship. No trust and no commitment to what they'd shared.

Taking her to dinner just meant he was a glutton for punishment.

Promise not to touch, she'd requested. Yes, that definitely was for the best. But his last remark to her had been wrong.

Not being able to clasp her hand with his and feel the connection he'd imagined they shared was his loss, not hers.

Will's choice of the small coffeehouse where they'd had their first date both surprised and pleased Natalie. The family-run business was off the beaten path, earthy, with great food and amazing coffee. It was one of those hole-in-the-wall places where you were just as likely to see a sport's star or other celebrity as you were to see your grocer or beautician.

The perfect eclectic blending of two worlds where everyone fit.

If he'd taken her somewhere else on that first date, somewhere where she'd have been expected to know what

fork went where or had to interact with the rich and fa-
mous, would she have let herself fall so madly in love
with him?

Let herself? Ha. As if she'd had a choice. Will had
stepped into her life, and she'd tumbled. There had been
no letting or conscious decision. Will had just happened.

As always, he was the perfect gentleman, opening
doors, pulling out her chair. But beneath the polished
exterior most wouldn't see past, she sensed his tension.
Tension that was perhaps caused by his care in making
sure he kept his promise to not touch.

She'd caught him pulling away twice during their walk
to the restaurant and wanted to cry both times. He'd often
put his hand at the small of her back or held her hand
when they'd walked together, and she'd sorely missed
that gesture.

He'd been right that his not touching her was her loss.

But she'd been just as right to insist that he keep his
hands to himself. She only had so much strength.

Unlike the present, that first dinner together had been
filled with excitement, anticipation and fun conversation
as they'd sat across from each other and gotten to know
one other. He'd taken her breath away when his hand
had covered hers on the table. That had been the first
time they'd skin-to-skin touched. Her hand stung from
the memory and she rubbed the area as if her flesh truly
burned. She should have known from the bold signet
ring he wore that he came from wealth. He'd not told her
his father was a senator, nor that his mother was worth
millions, if not billions. What was it he'd said? That his
father worked in government and his mother managed
a family business? What he had told her was that his favorite food was lasagna, he had a secret obsession with
watching old late-night sitcoms, that his mother had made

him learn to play the piano and that he'd done so to please her even though he'd been dreaming of kicking a ball into a net the whole time because he loved playing soccer. He'd recounted numerous tales of doing so, and admitted he'd continued to play during university and still played in the occasional friendly rivalry pickup game.

They'd talked about her parents, four older brothers, their wives and her numerous nieces and nephews. She'd told him how she'd worked from the moment she was old enough to get a job, kept her grades high enough to get a full scholarship, and proudly told him that she'd been the first person in her family to graduate from college. Sitting across from him, smiling at him, she'd felt as if they were having the most important conversation of their lives.

How ironic that they now sat across from each other in the same restaurant.

Oh, Will. Why did you bring me here, where it all started?

"Ninety-four!" Their order number was called.

"I'll get it," Will assured her when she started to rise, motioning for her to sit back down.

Leaning back in her chair, Natalie watched him go to the counter and smile at the attendant as he gathered their tray. When he turned, their gazes met and every emotion she'd ever felt for him zinged through her. Every desire. Every smile. Every bit of joy. Every hope and dream. Her heart broke from the joy of it, from the loss of him, and she had to look away before she lost her composure.

She understood how she could have just gone along with everything he wanted for so long. Even now she was tempted.

Setting the tray on their table, he settled back into his seat, but seemed more interested in watching her than in the food.

Natalie had forgone lunch because she'd been too nervous to eat, her stomach was protesting as it had been
doing a lot lately, and her food smelled delicious, so she
took a bite of her panini. The warm gooey cheese made
her mouth water. Hopefully, eating would settle the un-
easiness in her belly. Either way, the last thing she needed
was a lack-of-food hypoglycemic episode leaving her
fuzzy-headed. No telling what she'd do. Like beg him
to forgive her stupidity in moving out of his apartment
and zipping her lips on how she truly felt about so many
things in their relationship, such as his mother, and how
he'd chosen to go to so many family events alone, and
how being here with him filled her heart with such re-
morse for what they'd lost.

Trying to make sure she didn't choke on her food,
she chewed the bite thoroughly, self-conscious of every
movement of her mouth. When she'd swallowed it and
he'd yet to pick up his food, she asked, "What?"

"Just wondering how we reached this point."

Natalie paused, her panini midway to her mouth. "I
guess the way any couple's relationship fails, lack of com-
munication and growing apart."

"What happened around your birthday felt more of a
ripping apart." Watching her, he took a bite of his Cajun
spiced sandwich, taking his time as he slowly chewed.
"I didn't see it coming, so I felt blindsided."

Trying to figure out what to say, she toyed with her
food. Another wave of nausea hit hard. She set her sandwich down on her plate. A hypoglycemic episode would
be way preferable to throwing up.

"My leaving was the culmination of the issues in our
relationship that were there from the beginning, but had
festered and poisoned everything," she told him, push-

ing her plate back as now she couldn't stand the smell of her food.

He arched a brow. "We lived together for half a year and you never said a word about relationship issues, other than my mother. These issues hit you at your birthday party to the point you left without so much as a word to me, without our discussing them as two adults should. Instead, you moved out of our home?"

She flinched at his accusatory tone. She should have spoken up sooner. She should have talked with him about how she felt. How did she explain that she'd been afraid of losing him if she spoke up and made demands on their relationship? Pathetic.

"Your apartment is beautiful, Will, but it was never *my* home."

Progress. She'd made an admission, that being in the pristine apartment overlooking Central Park had often left her feeling as if she was checked into a sterile luxury suite rather than any sense of her belonging.

She'd felt like the poor little girl from Jersey, wearing hand-me-downs from the children her mother was paid to pick up after, and was there to play nice, or not allowed to play at all.

Will furrowed his forehead. "You lived there for six months. What was that? An extended vacation?"

His question echoed her thoughts, her feelings. Being with him had been like being on a dream vacation, an escape to a fantasy theme park where she ignored unpleasantries because she knew she had to eventually go back to reality. That feeling had kept her from ever relaxing enough to feel at home in his apartment or his life.

"It was my being at your beck and call for however long you were interested in me," she admitted, not quite believing she'd found the nerve to be so honest. "My living with you made our relationship convenient for you."

His face twisted with confusion. "But was somehow an inconvenience for you? Is that what you're saying? That living with me was a problem? That you didn't want to be there, and I coerced you into moving in with me?"

"No," she denied. When she'd first moved in with him she'd been wearing rose-colored glasses and everything had seemed wonderful with the exception of Rebecca's disapproval. "Not an inconvenience, but, looking back, it happened too soon and there were a lot of things we should have discussed first. We should have spent more time together before we took that step. We weren't ready to live together."

Her claim had doubt spreading across his handsome face. "Apparently, but not having to go back and forth between two places cut down on travel time so we could spend more time together. We were both ready for that."

"True." They'd been desperate for every precious second together.

"But you're saying the relationship issue that occurred to you at your birthday party is that you think things would have been better had we continued to travel between two residencies rather than having lived together?"

"Better?" She shrugged. "The obvious answer is no. But if I think back to the time we lived apart, then I recall you hungry to spend every spare moment with me and that's been gone from our relationship. At times over those past few weeks, you were so distracted it was as if you didn't even see me."

A flicker of guilt flashed on his face. A flicker that made her wonder what he wasn't telling her. He'd glossed over his dance with Stella, but was the woman's return the reason Natalie had felt he was keeping something from her?

"Besides all the things going on at the hospital and Harroway Industries and the foundation, it's an election year for my father," he pointed out, but his gaze didn't quite meet hers. "I'm expected to make an appearance at certain family and press functions. As an only child, it's important that I be there."

All true but none of the things he listed were the real cause of their problems. Or the cause of that guilty flash.

Her stomach growled. Lowering her gaze to her sandwich, she forced herself to take another bite and slowly chewed, hoping it stayed put. "The problem, since you seem oblivious to it, is that I'm not welcome to come with you."

His forehead furrowed. "There's nothing to be oblivious to because, for the most part, that's not true."

"Isn't it? How often was I included in those invites? How often did you bring me to those fancy Harroway dinners and campaign parties? To your mother's when she called and needed you to come running for her latest emergency on yet another of the few nights we had alone those last few weeks?"

The skin pulled tight over his cheekbones as his gaze narrowed. "I was under the impression you didn't want to go to my father's campaign events, to my mother's business dinners, that you didn't like the attention, and that you preferred I go as Mother's escort while you spent time with Callie or visiting with your family."

She couldn't deny his claim, but only because she'd been made to feel so unwelcome by Rebecca. She'd wanted to be with him, to be included and for him to be proud to have her at his side rather than worried that she was a cause of embarrassment as his mother had insinuated on more than one occasion.

"With the exception of private meetings with Mother, you were always welcome to attend, Natalie."

Natalie rolled her eyes. "You think your mother would have allowed that? That had you started showing up with me in tow that she wouldn't have let her displeasure be known?"

"I don't understand why you're always so negative about her." He genuinely looked confused. "She sensed how you felt, of course, but still reached out, like helping with your party because she wants me happy."

Natalie fought rolling her eyes, again. Rebecca wanted Will happy with someone of his own social status and any negativity Rebecca had sensed was her own. At least, initially. But, even at the end, Natalie had never said anything back to Rebecca out of respect for Will as she'd known it would upset him. She'd just silently suffered the woman's obvious disapproval, just as she'd stood there, watching Will and Stella, listening to Rebecca go on and on about them as if Natalie wasn't Will's live-in girlfriend right up until she'd realized she'd had enough.

And, rightly or wrongly, she'd ditched her own birthday party.

"You'd have to ask your mother on my reasons why I was so negative regarding her," Natalie suggested because she suspected nothing she said would convince Will.

"I'd rather you tell me." Will's phone began to ring. Pulling the sleek gadget from his pocket, he glanced at the screen. "It's my mother."

Of course it was. She probably had his phone tapped, listening in to their conversation the entire time, and had decided enough was enough.

Enough is enough, Natalie's insides screamed.

"Great. You can ask her what possible reason I could have for feeling negative toward her, but we both know she'll act as if she has no idea." Because Natalie knew the woman presented her feelings toward Natalie very differently to Will than she did directly to Natalie.

"Natalie." His tone held warning.

"Don't you dare tell me not to express my feelings, Will Forrest," she interrupted, anger filling her at just how long she'd let Rebecca play mind games with both her and Will. "You asked me here tonight for a reason. For us to talk. If it was to prove that I was wrong to leave—" leaning forward, chin high, she held his gaze and gestured to the phone he now held and was about to swipe "—then, don't answer that, and we can finish our conversation."

Why it was suddenly so important he not answer the phone at that particular moment wasn't exactly clear, but Natalie felt adamant in insisting he not answer.

Frowning, he glanced down at the lit-up screen. He looked torn, but rather than swipe to answer, he hesitated.

With bated breath, she waited to see what he'd do.

Eyes glittering, expression stern, he stared back, then set his phone down on the tabletop. "She's my mother, Natalie. I'm her only child. She's going to call, sometimes at inopportune times. She is a part of who I am. Is this what you want? What will make you happy? For me to ignore her, or push her out of my life because you don't like her?"

Stunned by his question, she fought to keep her jaw off the coffee shop floor. "When have I ever said I didn't like your mother because I know I've never said that?"

He harrumphed. "Some things are obvious."

How dare he act like she'd been the one to shun his

mother? To put the wedge between them? Rebecca had taken one look, turned up her snooty nose and not hidden her displeasure of their relationship to Natalie.

"She probably knows we're talking right now and that's why she called to interrupt." His gaze darkened. But now that the filter was off, her hurt was mingled with anger and pent-up frustrations poured from her. "She did a great job keeping you away from me the past month of our relationship. Why stop now?"

"You're wrong about her." His expression had grown terse, his lips pulling into a tight line. "But even if what you claim was true, what reason does she have to interrupt us at this point? You moved out weeks ago. Besides, if you weren't so prickly around her—"

"Prickly?" Natalie interrupted, her head starting to hurt. "The woman can't stand me and you're implying that's my fault? I met her with my arms wide-open and from the beginning she rejected me as being part of your life. She may have smiled and talked nice to you, but her teeth were bared when she looked my way. Why are we even here?"

Will took a deep breath, then quietly said, "Because once upon a time we had something special between us and now we don't even talk and that doesn't feel right."

Natalie's mouth opened, then she closed it as his sincerity defused her anger.

As frustrating as she found their situation, Will was a good man. Maybe he wanted to be "just friends," and that was what had prompted him to ask her to dinner. How could Natalie be "just friends" with someone who put her hormones into high gear and her heart into a vice?

Regardless, she didn't want to argue. Not because of a need to try to keep the peace, although that was there, too, but because being upset with him made her insides hurt. She didn't want to fight with Will.

"You're right. It doesn't feel right that we no longer talk." Understatement of the year. "You know how I feel about you," she said, determined that no matter what his reasons for being there were, that her reasons for coming were to be open and honest with him. "But my caring about you isn't enough. That's why I left. I want more."

She wanted him. As her partner. Her lover. Her everything. She wanted to not question her place in his life when other women flirted with him. When other women danced with him. She didn't want to feel the tug-of-war for his time and attention from his mother or wonder if someday he'd give in to Rebecca's desire for him to replace Natalie with someone "more fitting." Someone like Stella.

His phone started ringing again.

Sighing, Natalie's eyes dropped to where the offensive device sat on the table, then rose back up to Will. For once, he completely ignored his phone, his gaze intent on her instead.

"What more are you talking about, Natalie?" His eyes darkened to a deep green that cut into her. "Tell me how much it's going to cost me to get you back in my bed. We'll negotiate from there."

Cost him? Negotiate? He sounded so much like his mother that Natalie cringed. And *back in his bed*? Was that why he was there? Because of *sex*? She wanted his heart and he just wanted sex.

Fighting disappointment, she shook her head. "Nothing, Will. Our relationship—former relationship—isn't going to cost you anything." She lifted her napkin from her lap and placed it on the table. "Answer your mother."

His gaze narrowed. "Why are you being so stubborn?"

"Is that what you call my wanting to be treated with respect? As an equal in our relationship?" she countered.

"You're saying that I've treated you poorly? Or inferior in some way?" he scoffed, clearly not seeing her point.

"Not poorly, but not as your partner, either," she clarified, fighting to keep her voice from breaking as she spoke. She wished her head and emotions weren't such a jumbled mess. What was wrong with her? It was as if she couldn't think straight or keep her feelings in line for anything these days.

"My partner?" He leaned back, staring at her for long moments before he spoke again. "Is this some get-a-ring ploy? Is that what this past month has really been about? I won't be manipulated."

Realizing what he meant, Natalie gasped in horror. "Are you serious? Get-a-ring ploy? As if." Okay, so she had dreamed he'd someday want to marry her, but not because of a desire to manipulate him or anything other than to love him and share his life. The nerve. "Perhaps you've forgotten, but you're who asked for us to go to dinner. Not me," she reminded. "I've not asked for anything from you, *ever*," she also reminded. "And I never will. You must have me confused with one of your other ex-girlfriends."

His facial muscles tightened with displeasure. "There you go with more Stella accusations. Your lack of faith in my fidelity to you is disturbing."

His phone quit ringing but immediately started again. The sound grated on her nerves to the point Natalie could stand no more.

On the verge of spilling the tears rapidly accumulating in her eyes, or possibly taking his phone and flinging it across the café, Natalie gestured to the offending technology. "My 'lack of faith in your fidelity,' as you put it, no longer holds relevance. We're through with our relationship and this conversation, so answer your mother. She won't quit until you do."

With that, she rose from her chair to leave.

"Natalie!" He stood, reached out to stay her, his fingers firm around her wrist.

Her gaze dropped to where he held her, not hard, but with enough force that she'd have to jerk free to walk away.

The phone's blaring rang through her like an annoying reminder of why their relationship hadn't worked, would never work, and why no matter how much her heart and body said otherwise, she had to heed logic. Will cared for her. Natalie knew his feelings for her had been real. Although perhaps his back-in-his-bed comment hinted at where his feelings toward her really lay. She deserved to be loved, to be in a relationship where she stood on even ground with her partner. She'd never be that with Will. Not when his mother continuously interfered, fanning the flames of Natalie's insecurities, and Will was oblivious to how his mother affected Natalie and their relationship. He didn't even want to see but seemed to prefer being in denial.

They really were over.

She lifted her gaze to his.

"Don't touch me," she reminded.

His expression tightened, his eyes searching hers a brief moment, then his face became an unreadable cold mask that would make his mother proud.

"As you wish." Then he let her go.

CHAPTER THREE

"But I'm an ICU nurse," Natalie insisted the next morning when she arrived at the hospital for her regular shift to find that she'd been scheduled to work in the cardiovascular intensive care unit.

"Our census is down," her ICU nurse manager pointed out, not looking overly concerned that Natalie was in a near panic. "Theirs is up, and Connie is going to be out for a couple of weeks. You're already familiar with the patients from yesterday. It makes sense you'd be who we shifted to the unit for continuity of care."

"But…"

"No buts, Natalie. For the foreseeable future, you're covering for Connie."

Which is how Natalie ended up in the CVICU again that morning with two of Will's patients, Mattie Johnson and Donald Eastland, who was a new admit that morning after Will had performed an emergency coronary artery bypass graft on him in the wee morning hours. Mattie she could understand, but Natalie would have thought after the eagle eyes from the day before that Gretchen would have intentionally kept her away from any of Will's newly admitted patients. No such luck.

"You could check with some of the other ICU nurses to see if any of them wanted to trade. If you had someone lined up, wanting to be in CVICU, maybe they'd let you transfer out," Callie suggested, giving a look of commiseration as Natalie unlocked the medicine cart to get her morning medications for Mr. Eastland.

Natalie shook her head.

"I'm fine." If she said the words often enough, maybe she'd start believing them and feeling them, because stress was taking its toll. During the long restless night, she'd resigned herself to possibly never being fine again. Or at least not whole, because Will would always have a piece of her heart. "I am just going to have to toughen up and get over seeing him here. It sucks, but what choice do I have unless I want to change jobs?"

Callie gave a sympathetic look.

"Besides, whether I work with him, or not, I'm not going to escape seeing him." She didn't need the media for that, either. Every time she closed her eyes he was there. In her mind. In her heart. "We're both on the Children's Cancer Charity Gala committee, and unless he chooses not to come—" a distinct possibility as he'd already missed a few of the meetings "—then I'm going to have to learn to let my feelings for him go."

"The woes of dating someone like Dr. Forrest, I suppose," Callie mused, then cut her gaze to Natalie's and she lowered her voice conspiratorially. "He's coming up the hallway."

Natalie's heart skipped a beat as she steeled herself to the prospect of seeing Will. A Will that wasn't hers. That qualifier made all the difference. She'd held out a sliver of hope until he'd asked what it was going to cost him to get her back in his bed. Money. When had she ever asked him for anything? She wanted him. Not his money or his status. And she wasn't for sale. Her heart had been his for the taking, free of charge, but apparently all he'd really wanted was her body.

She wanted *him*. His time. His attention. His heart. All things she'd never have. The sooner she accepted that, the better. She couldn't start healing until she completely abandoned that hope.

Bracing herself, she turned, faced him and was shocked to see that he didn't look quite as well put together as Dr. William Harroway Forrest generally presented himself to the world. Although it was slight, there was a fatigue around his eyes that wasn't usually there, as if he'd had a rough night.

There she went again. Wanting to hope when none existed. He'd been called in to stent Donald Eastland in the early morning hours. Of course he looked tired. His weariness had nothing to do with her or how their dinner had ended.

"Here again, I see. Who's Mattie's nurse?" His tone was brusque, conveying his irritation that she was one of the first people he bumped into upon entering the CVICU.

She took a deep breath and steadied herself for their required interaction. She could do this. She had to do this. Unlike him, she needed her job.

"I am."

He nodded as if he'd expected that. Her own annoyance grew. It wasn't as if she wanted to be in the CVICU or that she'd arranged to be his patients' nurse. Besides, he should have known when he saw her that she'd been assigned to provide Mattie's care. If he didn't like it, maybe he should talk to management. They'd listen to him.

"The night nurse said Mattie had an uneventful night," she kept her tone level, professional. "Her vitals are consistent with how they were when I clocked out yesterday and she was stable when I was in her room just a few minutes ago."

"If she stays stable, I'll cut back on her medications in hopes of weaning her off the vent today. The sooner we get her back to breathing unassisted, the better."

Natalie nodded. She'd expected that as soon as Mattie was strong enough to breathe on her own he'd remove her intubation tube.

"I'll let you know if anything changes."

"You do that."

Natalie's gaze cut to his. Had his comment been laced with sarcasm? It was hard to fathom that it had been as Will wasn't one to make snide remarks. But that's what he'd just done.

Sensing the growing tension in their exchange and probably wanting to remind them that there were others around, Callie nudged her arm. "I'm off to check on my aortic aneurysm repair patient in room two. Yell if you need me or need to know where to find something."

Natalie smiled at her bestie. Thank goodness for her friend. Everything would be so much more difficult without her love, support and spare room to crash in while she figured out her next step.

Callie walked away, leaving Will and Natalie alone near the medication cart and he just stood there, staring at her as if he didn't know what to say. Natalie sighed. "Callie's not the only one who needs to check on her patients. It's time for Mr. Eastland's meds. Have a good day, Dr. Forrest."

Fighting a busting headache that throbbed at his temples, Will watched Natalie dart into Mr. Eastland's CVICU room. As if she sensed his gaze followed her, she drew the curtain, blocking his view through the glass wall that faced the nurses' station so the nurses could more easily keep a check on their critically ill patients.

He struggled to keep from marching into the room and pointing out that what he needed was for her to stop this nonsense. Nonsense such as calling him Dr. Forrest.

Her comments from the night before raced through his mind for what seemed like the millionth time. Not once had she previously said anything about not feeling at home in his condominium. He'd known she worried about the differences in the background, but he hadn't realized she didn't like their home. If she'd disliked their place, they could have looked for something more to her taste. The layout and the view had appealed to him, plus he'd been able to jog in Central Park, but he would have been fine with giving her carte blanche.

As far as his mother went, yes, he'd made a mistake in letting her put Natalie's party together, but he'd been thrilled she'd wanted to help, that yet again she was trying to reach out to Natalie. He suspected she'd called her event planner and had her invite the "usual" guest list, not thinking to add Natalie's friends and family. No wonder, with everything she had going on with her health and the company. It seemed the more his mother tried to build their relationship the more Natalie backed away from it.

It had been the only area of real contention in their relationship as far as he'd known, and he'd believed she'd eventually realize their financial differences didn't matter to him. Even with his mother, he'd thought their relationship would eventually improve. How could it not when they were the best women he'd ever known?

He'd thought Natalie didn't like going to his father's political events or his mother's business ones, so he'd purposely not pushed for her to when he always felt her discomfort, trying to shield her from the press and what-ever it was she feared so much. How was he to know she'd take that as his not wanting her there?

He'd wanted her there.

But he needed to get his head on straight. If Natalie cared so little that she could leave, be upset over his mother, over Stella when there was no longer anything between them, not even rationally talk things over before just disappearing from her birthday party and their home, then so be it. He needed to focus on helping his mother get well, anyway. That she refused surgery until after contracts were signed frustrated him. He understood her desire to do what was right by the company and their employees, but, selfishly, the company meant nothing to him if it cost him her. At least she'd agreed to go for localized radiation treatments in hopes of shrinking the mass, or at least keep it from growing while she delayed the mastectomy her specialist had recommended.

His mother beating her cancer was what he needed to focus on.

He was just finishing in Mattie's room when Natalie popped her head out of Donald Eastland's CVICU room.

"Good. I was hoping you were still here."

She actually did look relieved to see him. Her big brown eyes were filled with concern. He didn't fool himself that it was because of anything personal, and hadn't he just decided that was fine by him? They were through.

"I know you probably planned to, anyway, but do you mind listening to Mr. Eastland's chest before you go?" she asked. "I don't like what I'm hearing in his lower lobes."

He might question her good senses on moving out, but Natalie's nursing skills were top-notch. He trusted her patient assessments implicitly. She had a good ear and her nursing instincts were on the money. They'd only worked together a handful of times prior to the day before, but she'd always impressed him with her quick mind and healing touch.

"What's up?" he asked as he stepped just inside the room, disinfected his hands, his stethoscope, then donned gloves and a mask before moving closer to his patient's bed.

"Soft rales heard anteriorly and posteriorly in the lower lobes bilaterally," she told him, pulling the sheet back to uncover the patient's chest, exposing the heart monitor lead dotting his chest. "I wasn't sure if you planned to round on him prior to heading to clinic, but believed you'd want to listen for yourself and order a chest X-ray."

Will placed his stethoscope diaphragm to Mr. Eastland's chest and listened for the soft crackle in the man's lower lung lobes. He immediately heard the abnormal noises and frowned.

"It's quick for post-op pneumonia to have set in," he mused, doing a quick assessment for fluid retention. His patient's left leg had plus two non-pitting edema. His right leg had plus one swelling. Neither side was necessarily unexpected following the removal of a femoral vein on his left leg to graft in his heart to bypass the blockage, but Will appreciated Natalie's quick assessment. The sooner a problem was caught the less damage it was likely to cause. "Good call. I definitely want that chest X-ray. Draw labs on him, too, including a BNP, complete blood count, comprehensive metabolic profile and a D-dimer, just in case. I may end up ordering a CT of his chest, but I'll see what these show and go from there."

Concern flickered in her eyes. "Surely, you won't have two patients throw clots on back-to-back days."

"I hope not." His patient statistics were better than average, but when dealing with the human body anything could, and often did, happen. "Make all his tests STAT and let me know the minute they're available."

Already logging into the computer system to enter the orders, Natalie nodded. "I'll keep a close check on him and will keep you updated."

Taking another listen to his patient's chest, Will watched Natalie type and hated the ache that settled into the pit of his stomach. They were through. How could he look at her and miss that she was no longer there when he got home when he knew she didn't want to be there? Perhaps if he had told Natalie what was going on with his mother, it would have made a difference. That despite the strong front she put on, he was terrified he was going to lose her and wished she'd step away from the company she loved and focus on her health.

His heart squeezed. He'd been so caught up in worrying about his mother he probably had taken Natalie for granted those last few weeks they'd been together. But shouldn't he have been able to count on her to be there for him even when he was distracted?

Perhaps sensing his gaze, she glanced up, their eyes meeting as she caught him watching her. But rather than say anything, she swallowed a bit nervously, then returned her attention to the computer screen without comment.

Best thing he could do was forget her and move on with his life. It's what he'd done when Stella had left. She'd betrayed his faith in her by taking off to Paris when he'd thought they were serious. He'd been fine. He'd be fine again. Only, this time felt different. His insides felt more raw, more betrayed, more panicked to undo whatever had made Natalie leave him so she'd return to their life together. Probably because of what was going on with his mother and how that already had his personal life on edge.

Getting over Natalie might take a long time, he thought later that morning when his phone pinged with a text message from her while he was seeing patients in clinic for follow-up. It was probably a Pavlovian response, but when he glanced at his smart watch and saw her name, his heart sped up, pounding his pulse in his ears. It wasn't as if he thought the message was personal. Whatever her real reasons, she felt it necessary that their relationship end. So be it.

He glanced at the message on his watch. Donald Eastland's chest X-ray showed infiltrates in both lower lobes. His white blood cell count had been normal. His D-dimer was still pending.

"Get a CT of his chest. With and without contrast," Will said out loud, his phone taking the message and sending it at his voice command.

Yes, sir, came her immediate reply.

Will winced at her formal response, then berated himself for doing so. What did he expect? For her to still put smiley faces and hearts in her messages to him? He'd never been a mushy kind of guy, hadn't really thought much about her emojis, but the barren reply felt like another slap in the face in a long string of them over the past few days.

Maybe someday he'd get a text from Natalie and his body wouldn't react any differently than it would to a text from any other nurse taking care of his patients.

Maybe.

"Good morning, Mrs. Johnson," Natalie greeted her patient. She greeted every patient every morning as if she expected a response. Sometimes she got one. Sometimes she didn't.

"It's shaping up to be a beautiful day. A bit cold, though," she continued as she moved about the room.

Mattie's dark eyes watched her closely.

"I imagine you're ready for that ventilation tube to come out today."

Mattie's head nodded ever so slightly.

"Dr. Forrest was hoping he'd be able to remove it yesterday, but you never roused enough for him to feel he should. Maybe today will be the day. How are you this morning?" Natalie held out the nine-by-nine dry erase board and a marker to the woman.

Been better.

Natalie smiled. "True. You've been worse, too, but Dr. Forrest has you on the mend and hopefully you'll be ready to go home soon."

The woman gave another slight nod.

Natalie explained each medication as she administered it via Mattie's intravenous line.

Next, she gave her patient a sponge bath, taking care to be gentle as she cleaned her frail skin and then applied lotion. When Natalie was done, she made sure the sheet covered Maddie's freshly bathed body.

"I'll get someone to help me and be back in a bit to get you onto clean bedding," she promised, turning to leave the CVICU room.

She came to a quick stop just outside the privacy curtain.

"Will…er… Dr. Forrest," she corrected herself, cheeks heating. Would she ever be able to see him and not feel the personal connection between them? To not think of him as Will, the man who'd wooed her, and wowed her, and ended up breaking her heart? "Good morning."

She'd do her best to greet him with the same respect she showed every hospital employee. Just because Will was the most beautiful man she'd ever seen and she'd once kissed every inch of him didn't change the fact that he was her colleague.

Just because he used to be hers and her body didn't understand that he no long was didn't change that. Just because...

Natalie swallowed, then refocused her thoughts. "I was on my way to grab Callie or one of the other nurses to help me change Mattie's bedding."

"I'll help you," he surprised her by offering.

Natalie bit into her lower lip. Refusing his help would mean delaying getting Mattie onto fresh bedding. Maybe he was just as helpful with all his patients. She suspected that was the case. Just because he'd flunked out on being her Prince Charming didn't mean he wasn't a fantastic doctor, person and coworker.

"Okay."

Together they untucked the lift sheet, then slid Mattie to the far side of the bed, taking care to keep the loose top sheet over her for her privacy. When they'd accomplished that, Natalie undid the old sheet, then made up half the bed with the clean linens.

"If you'll raise her feet and hang on to the old sheet, I'll slide it back over the new," Will offered.

Together they got the soiled bedding all removed and Mattie situated. Natalie put on the woman's fresh hospital gown, then replaced the top sheet while Will talked to Mattie, explaining what her latest set of labs and vitals had revealed, while holding the woman's hand.

Fighting the aww moment his gesture of kindness and comfort sent through her, Natalie bagged up the soiled linens. She'd seen how he was with other patients in the past, with his mother. The man had a heart of gold. If only he could have given that heart to Natalie.

"Your oxygen saturations dipped some with all the moving around of getting clean," Will told his patient. "I'm not convinced that you're ready to go off the ventilator yet."

Mattie grunted, making her disapproval of his comment plain.

"Maybe later," he offered with an empathetic pat to her hand, reminding Natalie yet again that the reasons she'd fallen for him had gone far beyond their sexual chemistry. "I'll check back after I finish in clinic and will keep my fingers crossed that you're strong enough for it to happen soon."

Mattie wrote "Okay" on her board, and then, a disappointed look on her face, she closed her eyes. Within seconds, she was asleep, the exertion from being bathed having taken its toll.

"She looks better today," Natalie mused watching the rise and fall of the woman's chest as she tucked the covers around her.

"She does. I was hoping she'd be improved enough to come off the vent, though. Maybe I'll reconsider when I check on her this evening."

Natalie turned, expecting to see Will staring at his patient. Instead, his gaze was trained on her. Heat flooded her face and, self-conscious, she quickly glanced away and walked over to the curtain that provided the room with a bit of privacy through the heavy glass walls. She pulled the curtain back so she'd be able to see into the room from the nurses' station.

And then they were both just standing there.

"I should go check on my other patient."

Snapping out of whatever it was that had held his eyes to her, he nodded. "Me, too."

Which meant they were headed in the same direction.

"How is Mr. Eastland this morning? Urine output good? Oxygen saturation holding? His swelling any better?" Will asked in rapid-fire succession as he disposed of his used personal protective equipment then disinfected his hands and stethoscope.

"The night nurse reported that he remained stable with no episodes or evidence of reoccurring fluid overload. His vitals have been good this morning and he was asking if he'd be able to eat today," she. Wow. Her voice sounded normal. How was that even possible when being near Will made her insides ache so? When her heart was screaming in frustration?

"Good to hear," he answered, oblivious to her inner turmoil that they were carrying on a conversation as if they had never been anything more than coworkers. As if they'd never meant anything at all to each other. "If everything appears okay when I check him, I'll change his nothing-by-mouth orders to a liquid diet and we'll advance him as tolerated."

Trying to force her mind to focus on their patient, Natalie nodded. "He'll be glad to hear that."

"If his vitals remain good, he'll transfer to a step-down unit later today, and hopefully be home within a couple of days at most."

She'd suspected as much when the night nurse had given a good report on the CABG patient that morning. Good. That would be one less patient she and Will would have to communicate over. Maybe her manager would be kind and make sure her next assignment belonged to another physician.

While Will went to check on Mr. Eastland, Natalie

dropped off the dirty laundry. First peeping through the glass wall into the room to make sure Mattie was still resting okay, Natalie then disinfected herself and donned appropriate PPE prior to entering Mr. Eastland's room to see if Will needed her assistance.

The man was sitting up in his bed, smiling and talking with Will. Amazing what a few bypassed blocked arteries and some diuretics could do to improve a person's life outlook.

Hearing her enter the room, Will turned her way, his lips automatically curving in a smile. That is, until he seemed to remember all the reasons why he shouldn't, and his smile disappeared as quickly as it had happened.

His smile disappearing was like going from brilliant sunshine to being banned to the darkest dungeon. A chill prickling her skin, Natalie quivered at the drop in room temperature.

She could do this, she mentally prepped herself. She had to.

Natalie stepped in Mr. Eastland's CVICU room and Will's world immediately lightened. But that joy only lasted for a moment before it was replaced with the recall that Natalie wasn't his any longer.

He wavered between frustration and resignation that maybe he was meant to just remain single.

Being single didn't set one up for disappointment and betrayal.

But it did leave him lonely at night when he got into the bed he'd shared with Natalie. At times, he'd swear he could smell her favorite scented lotion, could hear her breathing next to him.

Yeah, he'd just stay single.

Not that his mother agreed. It was barely past 8:00 a.m.

and already she was texting to find out his dinner plans. No doubt any invitations issued would include Stella since he'd declined her invitation the prior day. Subtlety wasn't in his mother's nature and she was worried about him. Maybe he shouldn't have been so open with her about his breakup with Natalie. He should have known she'd try to patch up that part of his life by pushing him and Stella together, saying she'd rest easier knowing he had someone special in his life.

He'd had someone special in his life and look where that had gotten him.

Besides, even if he did decide to date again, it wouldn't be with a woman who'd proven she couldn't stick around any better than Natalie had. Losing Stella had never left him feeling gutted. When he saw her, he didn't fill with longing and have memories pulling him toward her.

Turning back to Mr. Eastland, Will fought to keep his sigh from escaping by retrieving his stethoscope from his pocket to listen to the man's chest. He went through his check, making sure pulses were good in all four extremities, that his swelling was decreased, his lungs cleared from the day before noises and that the man truly was as spry as he appeared.

"You going to send me home, Doc?"

"Not today."

"I feel a lot better," his patient pointed out, his dark gaze watching Will's every move.

"You look a lot better, too, and I intend to make sure it stays that way for at least another night. If you continue to do well today, I'll discharge you home tomorrow. For today, if there's a bed available, you'll be transferred to a regular hospital room, otherwise, you'll stay here for the duration of your stay."

The man nodded as if he'd had no true thoughts of going home that evening but had asked anyway.

Will and Natalie left Mr. Eastland's room together.

As they both reached up to disinfect, their hands touched, then immediately jerked away from each other, but not before Will felt the same shot of awareness touching Natalie always gave him. Apparently, his libido didn't care that their relationship had ended.

"Is this how it's going to be from now on?" he asked, fighting to keep his agitation under control. He'd cared about her, asked her to live with him. He'd dived in, opened his home to her, been crazy about her, and she'd turned her back on him. How could he have been so foolish?

Her gaze shot to him. "What do you mean?"

"This awkward silence and jerk-away reactions if we accidentally touch?"

Her brows drew together as she regarded him. "I can't imagine that we could ever be just friends, can you?"

He hadn't done anything deserving of her shutting him out of her life.

"No, I suppose not," he ground out, wondering how he could have been so wrong about her, about them. He walked away, gutted more than he should still be a month after she'd left him, but determined that he was done with Natalie Gifford.

CHAPTER FOUR

"Oh! I wasn't expecting to see you here."

Natalie's wide-eyed gaze had already clued Will in to that as they arrived at the conference room of the New York City Children's Cancer Charity office at the same time.

Will took a deep breath. Did she think he'd skip out because they were no longer together? Due to his mother's illness, he'd missed a few meetings, but he'd been a part of the organization for years. Now that cancer had personally touched his family he couldn't imagine not participating. If anything, he'd be pushing for the Harroway Foundation to increase their donations and involvement in organizations fighting cancer for these kids and their families, plus expanding what the foundation was doing for breast cancer research.

"I'm a board member representative on the committee," he reminded, aggravated at her accusatory tone. "The only times I miss a meeting are when it's unavoidable."

"Of course. It's just you've not been here the last few times, so I..." Her words died away and she sighed. "Never mind. The more the merrier, right?"

With that, she gave a tight smile, which might have been more of a grimace, then took off to find a seat.

Rather than follow, Will stood back, watching as she did a quick assessment of available seats. It wasn't lost to him that she chose one sandwiched between two places that appeared to be already occupied based upon the young mother sitting at one, and the pad of paper, pen and half-full water glass at the other.

The committee consisted of twenty people and were a diverse group from various walks of life. Some, like Will, were mostly there for their financial resources or board positions. Others like Natalie were doing the bulk of the organizing and legwork. And, then there were those who represented the group meant to be benefitted: children with cancer and their families.

Long before his mother's diagnosis, oncology had been a field dear to Will's heart. During residency he'd considered pediatric oncology as his focus after completing a short rotation, but cardiology had been his true love. One of his medical school buddies who had chosen to treat cancer in kids stopped him inside the doorway, a smile on his always friendly face.

"Will, good to see you." Lee shook his hand and they caught up on mutual acquaintances for a few minutes. "There's an empty seat on the other side of me. I'll slide over and you can sit next to Natalie."

Which meant his friend hadn't heard that he and Natalie were no longer together. What had Natalie told the man at past meetings when Will had been absent? Or had she just changed the subject anytime he was mentioned?

Glancing around the small meeting room, Will considered his seating options. There was only one other empty chair in the room and that one was next to Gregory Kendall. Will didn't have the patience for the man's stories about his greatness and prowess this evening. Or any evening, really, but Gregory's father was a longtime family acquaintance so Will had been enduring his over-flowing trust fund arrogance for years.

"Thanks, Lee." He wouldn't not sit by someone he liked so that he could sit by someone he barely tolerated just because Natalie happened to be in the opposite chair. He'd just ignore her. No big deal.

"Hello, Natalie," Lee greeted her, sliding his belongings over one seat before Will could stop him.

"Hi, Dr. Lewis," Natalie responded with a brief look upward before going back to staring down at the note-book she'd placed on the meeting table as if the blank pages had her in a trance. She didn't look up as Will pulled out his chair and sat next to her. How awkward to be so close physically and so distant emotionally to someone who'd so recently occupied such an important role in his life.

The entire office space was tiny, and the meeting room barely fit all the committee members. If Will wasn't care-ful he'd end up bumping again. Refusing to look her way, he turned toward Lee and asked how his practice was going.

Lee's forehead furrowed as he realized something had gone wrong in paradise. Will shook his head, indicating he didn't want to discuss it. Not ever, but definitely not with Natalie sitting next to him. Fortunately, Lee gave an understanding nod and most likely assumed they were having a lovers' quarrel. Lee would realize soon enough that they were done.

Something his body was struggling with as he caught a whiff of the scented lotion she used when not working at the hospital.

His insides knotted as flashbacks of rubbing the lotion onto her slender back, her thighs and calves as she lay naked on their bed filled him. She'd rolled over, looked up at him with eyes full of passion and adoration as she'd taken the lotion bottle from him, then pulled him to her and kissed him so thoroughly he'd trembled. Had that been two months ago? Three? Or longer?

Certainly, over the past few weeks of their relationship he'd been tired and torn emotionally with worry over his mother, wondering if her strong spirit would be enough to help her overcome her cancer, and if a son could love his mother through her treatments to see her ultimately cured. How many nights had he gone to bed those last few weeks and immediately drifted to sleep without making love to the beautiful woman next to him? He should have held her every night he'd had the chance. Made love to her until they'd both drifted to sleep sated and in each other's arms.

Unable not to, he glanced Natalie's way, his gaze colliding with hers. There was no way for her to know where his thoughts were, or that her scent was driving his desire through the roof with sensual memories. Her breath caught, her cheeks flushed and her eyes widened just a little before her long lashes swept down to hide anything that shone there.

The meeting started. Katrina Matthews, a full-time employee of the charity, stood and spoke for a few minutes, thanking everyone for coming as this was the last scheduled meeting prior to the gala. When Katrina finished the introduction to the night's agenda, as the cochair of the gala benefit, Natalie stood and handed out papers from a folder she'd had tucked beneath her notepad.

"The gala is fast approaching. For the most part, everything is coming together and running smoothly," she began, pushing a long red hair tendril behind her ear as she continued. "On the handout, I've listed where we stand on food, donations, etcetera, and included our planned timeline for the evening. If you will please take a moment to look it over and let me know of any corrections that need to be made, that would be wonderful."

They ran through the night's schedule, what they hoped to accomplish, and addressed a few last-minute concerns.

"Donations are lower than this time prior to last year's gala," the charity's other board member in attendance commented, glancing up over the rim of his reading glasses as he tapped a section on the handout. "Is that being looked into to ensure this year's event is viewed as a success?"

Natalie glanced toward Katrina, who gestured for her to continue. "We are aware donations are down. As with many charities, world events have strained corporate donations. We've reached out to several companies who've been generous in the past. Unfortunately, we've yet to hear back, but hopefully we will have prior to the gala and will have good news on those fronts."

"Times have been tough financially on a lot of places," a committee member pointed out. "We should be contacting more than just our same benefactors. Someone should generate a list of corporate charities and what their qualifications are, and if we fit, then apply for us to be considered. If we're lagging behind this year, we need to up what we're doing. Our cause is an important one."

"Good point," Natalie praised, then looked the man square in the eyes. "Would you like to volunteer for the position, Mr. Felix?"

The man quickly shot down that idea and everyone else in the room seemed too busy to take on the last-minute additional efforts to increase funds.

Will was willing to make a few calls to old family friends that should rally up their total by several thousand, but his time was too stretched already to take on heading the project. He'd work behind the scenes to help and, as in the past, would make a sizable donation. The more cancer research and support for families affected by it, the better.

When no one volunteered, Natalie said, "I agree that it's a worthy idea and I will do what I can to see it to fruition. Is anyone able to meet with me to do some research, fill out applications and possibly make some calls? We could meet here one day later this week or early next."

"I'll help."

Will's gaze shot to Gregory. Lee might not have heard about the breakup, but the man grinning at Natalie knew. Knew and was leering at her overtly. The man truly disgusted Will in ways that had nothing to do with the surge of fury hitting him in response to the way Gregory gobbled up Natalie with his eyes.

That was why Will's fingers had clenched, causing his grandfather's signet ring to dig into his flesh, not because Will felt any type of jealousy or protectiveness over Natalie. They'd been apart for a month. What she did was none of his business.

"Will and I want to help, too," Lee added, nudging him with his elbow as he spoke.

Will frowned at his friend. What was Lee saying? He'd thought Lee had figured out that he and Natalie were at odds. The last thing Will wanted was to interact with Natalie even more than necessary. With her scheduled indefinitely in the CVICU, work was difficult enough.

But as his gaze returned to Gregory eyeing her, Will corrected himself. The last thing he wanted was for Natalie to be stuck alone with that pompous Lothario.

Not that she couldn't handle herself or that Will had any say in how she spent her time. But Gregory was a smooth operator with a history of fooling even some of the city's most seasoned beauties. Regardless of what had happened between them, Natalie was a sweet, good person who'd had limited experience going into her relationship with Will. It was only natural that he wouldn't want her to be taken advantage of by the slick man.

He wanted to punch the man in the face, but maybe that was only natural, too, since a month didn't seem nearly long enough to be accustomed to the fact that Natalie was no longer his girlfriend.

Not that he'd ever had that problem in the past. Not even with Stella, who he'd once assumed he'd marry. When she'd broken his trust and taken off for Europe, he'd certainly not felt as if a hole had been torn in his chest.

"It's for a good cause," Lee declared, elbowing him again, not appearing bothered by Will's frown, as if Will wasn't catching the fact they were saving Natalie from Gregory. Apparently, Lee's vibes about the man were the same as Will's. But his friend was missing the point that it was no longer his place to rescue Natalie.

His gaze shifted to hers, and when they met, emotion sucker punched him.

She'd rather deal with Gregory's advances than spend time with him.

Her eyes instantly lowered, and, reeling from the realization of how different life could be in such a short amount of time, Will leaned back in his chair.

Not so long ago he'd seen himself growing old with Natalie, spending his life with her. Maybe he should have told her that. Maybe it was better, given the circumstances, that he hadn't.

Staying away from her was the best thing for him,

and her, too. He just needed to say he was already over-extended and to find someone else.

But there had always been something about Natalie that pulled him in. Sitting next to her, watching her take charge of the meeting and continue to grow with the confidence she seemed to exude in every aspect of her life—with the exception of him, apparently—he filled with pride at how far she'd come from when he'd first encouraged her to volunteer with the organization.

Looking at her, he knew that despite how their relationship had failed Natalie was a rare flower just waiting to blossom and stun the world with her inner and outer beauty.

He'd been damn lucky to have played even the tiniest role in her life, and even luckier to have gotten to so closely behold her magnificence.

And as much as logic said they'd never work, that he should stay away from her, he wasn't sure he could do that.

Or that he even wanted to.

One thing he was positive on, though, was that no way was he allowing Gregory Kendall alone time with Natalie.

Speak up and deny what Dr. Lewis just said, Natalie willed the silent man sitting next to where she stood.

Why wasn't Will vocalizing some great reason why he couldn't, or wouldn't, help with the mini project? Lord knew he could choose from a dozen excuses why he didn't have time to take on yet another endeavor. No one would judge a cardiac surgeon harshly for saying no to the volunteer project when he already did so much for so many personally and through the Harroway Foundation.

Surely, any moment he'd list one of the reasons he couldn't help.

But rather than wiggle off the hook Lee had put him upon, Will nodded. "Sure. Why not?"

As if he didn't know why not. She glared at him. She'd not wanted him to be the one to volunteer. Having to see him at the hospital each time she went in was enough to keep her stomach in tight knots, as it was. She didn't need extra time with him via the gala fundraising event.

"Between the three of us reaching out to those in our inner circles," he continued, his green gaze avoiding hers as he glared at Gregory Kendall, "I suspect pre-event donations will exceed last years and no one will question the event's success."

Was he trying to rescue her or torture her? Regardless, Natalie knew his increased involvement would be a good thing for the charity, and wasn't that her ultimate goal?

"No doubt," Lee agreed, grinning at Will. "Chump change to your inner circle. We got this."

Will ignored the comment, which didn't surprise Natalie. She'd never known him to make a big deal of his background. Sad that it had still played such a key role in driving a wedge between them.

Or his mother alone had done that. Had Rebecca pushed him to not include Natalie in social functions? Or had Will truly believed she'd not wanted to go and that he'd been doing her a favor by attending alone and leaving her to spend her time as she chose with friends and family? Or maybe Natalie's own insecurities about her background had caused the rift that had prevented her from ever truly trusting in their relationship. Most likely it had been a nasty combination that had knocked so many holes in her happiness and her ability to feel as if she belonged in Will's world.

Which was too bad because she missed him. The Will who would roll over and grin at her first thing in the morning. The Will who had kissed her and spun her around when she'd agreed to move in with him as if she'd made him the happiest man in the world. The Will who'd reach over and hold her hand as they drifted off to sleep. She missed that Will and couldn't help but wonder if they would still be together if he'd just been a cardiac surgeon meeting a nurse.

What was she doing?

Now was not the time for another round of twenty questions on why she and Will had failed as a couple. Time for that had come and gone. A month had passed. She needed to get over Will, although she suspected he would always hold a big chunk of her heart. How could any man ever take his place when Will was in so many ways the total package?

If only he'd loved her, been willing to take her side or at least acknowledge her concerns about his mother as legitimate.

If only she could quit thinking about him.

Forcing herself to refocus, Natalie thanked all three men, then moved on to the next question presented by a committee member. When they'd gone through everything on her portion of the agenda and the concerns raised, she thanked everyone for coming and turned the meeting over to her cochair.

Keeping her eyes on Katrina as the woman rose to speak, Natalie sat down, bumping against Will when she did. Although their clothes prevented skin-to-skin contact, the interaction had her knees wobbling and her head spinning. "Sorry," she mumbled, straightening her notebook to give her hands something to do to cover her discomfort. Once upon a time she'd sought any excuse to touch him, had thrilled that she'd had the right to run her hands over his body. Now she apologized for an accidental bump. Oh, how that made her heart grieve.

"No problem. Happens all the time."

Surprised at his light, almost teasing response, Natalie's gaze shifted to him.

"Women bumping into me accidentally," he clarified. His eyes were trained on Katrina, but she'd swear his lips had just twitched as if he found the incident humorous.

"It was an accident," she defended in a whisper, not sure why she felt the need, but not willing to let him imply she'd touched him on purpose.

"Sure. No problem." His tone suggested he didn't believe her.

Confused by his comment and determined she was going to just ignore him, she attempted to focus on what Katrina was saying.

To no avail, though, as her attention wandered back to the man sitting next to her. Did he realize his leg was close enough to hers that she could feel his body heat? That all she had to do was move her leg a hair's breadth and they'd be bumping against each other again?

His body heat enveloped her. As did his scent. It was all she could do not to breathe in the familiar spicy male fragrance that tempted her with memories of nuzzling against his neck in the early morning hours. She had lain awake so many nights, cradled against him, counting her lucky stars that she was there in his arms.

Why had she let the doubting demons inside her rob her joy? Why hadn't she felt she had a right to stand up to his mother and demand Will acknowledge her place in his life rather than watch their relationship erode because she'd been too afraid to fight for it? To fight for him?

Why? Because she'd grown up poor and his parents

were on a first-name basis with iconic American founding families. But ultimately, Will was still just a man to her woman. She'd worked so hard to overcome her poor beginnings, determined she wouldn't live just above poverty, but perhaps what she'd really needed to work on was how she mentally saw herself.

And how she saw him.

She inhaled and her senses filled further with Will, causing her to shift in her seat. Her knee brushed against his thigh and lightning shot through her. She reflexively jerked away. Her eardrums thrummed. The only thing she could hear was the pounding of her heartbeat, which seemed to be playing a tune devoted to him.

Will. Will. Will.

"Hmm?"

Natalie blinked. Good grief. Had she said his name out loud?

Noticing that all committee member eyes were on her, she realized she had. Her face caught fire as complete mortification hit.

"*Will* there be an opportunity for any of the special guest children and their family members to be recognized?" she asked, grasping at straws to cover her blunder. A stupid question as she knew the answer, they all did, but less stupid than admitting the truth: she'd said the man's name out loud because he'd overpowered her senses.

"We've always recognized the children we invite and their families," Katrina reminded, her brow furrowing at the interruption. Her look clearly said Natalie's question made no sense.

"Oh, sorry," she apologized, knowing her cheeks were a bright ruddy color. "This is my first year being involved."

"No problem," Katrina commented, then moved on through the items she wanted to cover prior to the meeting ending.

Will leaned over and whispered, "Nice cover, but I recognized your tone and what you just did. Want to tell me what you were really thinking?"

Rather than answer, she narrowed her eyes, then turned away from him to write some notes on her legal pad. How dare he make fun of her for being so stupid as to say his name? For being so weak her brain turned to mush when she was near him? Then again, with a mistake that ridiculous maybe she deserved to be made fun of.

She ordered herself to not look at Will, not think about Will, and to definitely not say his name out loud during a meeting ever again.

No matter how devoted he was to the Children's Cancer Charity, any hope Will had of paying attention to Katrina was shot the moment Natalie said his name.

Not that he'd been having much luck prior to that.

Being near Natalie was a distraction under the best of times.

She might have fooled the others with her gala question, but the rosy color to her cheeks divulged it had been a cover. What had she been thinking when she'd said his name? That she wished she was anywhere but next to him because his nearness was affecting her the way her nearness was affecting him?

His body had instantly recognized her tone. Longing had been evident in how she'd said his name and he'd zinged to life.

Convincing his body that their chemistry should have fizzled out the moment she turned her back on their relationship seemed impossible. Especially when she was mere inches from him and everything in him had sensed her beckoning him long before her lips had murmured his name.

Just the memory of their bodies entwined had Will swallowing. He had to stop, or he'd be the one with rosy cheeks from embarrassing himself in front of the others. He'd never been one to embark in a relationship based solely on physical attraction. Never had. Couldn't imagine that he ever would. Sex with Natalie had never just been about physical attraction, anyway. She'd always made him glad he was a man, glad to be alive and the recipient of her smiles.

His gaze lowered to her notebook and, his breath catching, he tensed.

She'd written his name and doodled around it.

They were supposed to be over as a couple. They were over. So what was she doing? Toying with him? Flirting with him? Letting him know she was as torn about being near him as he was her?

It took him only a millisecond to realize she drew without conscious thought to what she was doing as her eyes were trained on her cochair. As he watched her continue to mindlessly trace her pen over his name, his brain raced, trying to decipher the past week's events. He'd gone from confident in their relationship to crushed at her lack of commitment. Had he learned nothing from his relationship with Stella? He'd gotten too caught up too quickly with Natalie and made some bad choices, like asking her to live with him. He'd surprised himself as much as her when his question had slipped out of his mouth. He'd never lived with a girlfriend, but once the seed had been planted in his mind, he'd acknowledged living with Natalie was the perfect solution.

He'd wanted her there when he closed his eyes at

night, when he woke up in the mornings, when he came home. What was it she'd said? That his apartment had never felt like home to her. It sure hadn't felt like home to him since she'd moved out. He could barely stand to be there, seeing her and some memory everywhere he looked, hearing the echo of something she'd said, her laughter. The less time he was there these days, the better.

Maybe the stress of the past few months was getting to him. His mother finding her lump, confiding in him before she'd told anyone, including Will's father. Her swearing him to secrecy to protect Harroway Industries. His taking her to multiple specialist appointments as testing was performed and treatment decisions made. Work had always been his passion but was busy, with more early-morning calls summoning him to the hospital. And going from thinking his relationship with Natalie was solid to having it ripped away from him.

You let her go, an inner voice reminded him. *You were so caught off guard that she'd leave you that you let her go without putting up a fight to keep her.*

Had he asked her to stay, for them to work on the things that bothered her, would she have reconsidered?

If he'd told her about his mother, explained why he'd let his attention to their relationship slip, would she have wrapped her arms around him and promised him everything was going to be okay?

Natalie would swear that Will's leg had just brushed against hers on purpose. Rather than jerk away, his leg had lingered, the warmth searing her flesh.

She turned to look at him, meaning to frown as she shifted her leg away from his. He stared straight ahead as if completely caught up in the remaining details of the gala that Katrina was laying out.

Surely, he saw her from his peripheral vision, but if so, he ignored her, and she was making a spectacle of herself continuing to look at him.

Sighing, she turned away, telling herself she needed to pay attention and take notes on what Katrina was saying so she could clarify anything she didn't feel was clear.

Although most of the committee members were alumni, Natalie really was a newbie with a lot to learn. Glancing down, her eyes lit on what she'd written so far. Her lips parted and her stomach fisted.

Oh. No.

Will's name with scribbles around it.

What was wrong with her? Had she reverted to a love-sick teenager?

Trying not to attract attention, she flipped over her notepad. Unfortunately, she dropped her pen onto the table with a loud clang that once again had everyone in the room looking her way. Great.

"Sorry," she mumbled, mortified that she was caus-ing a disturbance during the meeting and because she'd drawn Will's name. Had he seen?

Please let him not have noticed.

This was difficult enough without embarrassing her-self that way.

She fought to keep from looking his way. She just couldn't.

If he'd seen, was he laughing at her? Probably. Poor, silly Natalie who couldn't be near him without making a fool of herself. Would he make a joke about women ac-cidentally writing his name, as well?

And why, dear heavens, was his thigh brushed up against hers again? Was he trying to torture her? Or just singe her skirt to her flesh from his heat?

When the meeting adjourned, Natalie longed to make

a beeline for the door, but as cochair, she had to stick around to answer questions.

Unfortunately, Gregory kept firing them off her way.

"Maybe we should go to dinner to discuss how I can best serve you," he offered, his tone leaving no doubt as to how he'd like to serve. He waggled his bushy dyed blond brows. "You'd be impressed at how handy I can be."

Gag. Was the tanning booth bronze guy serious? His handsy-ness was what concerned her. Concerned and repulsed. Currently, she couldn't imagine wanting to ever date again, but even if she could, Gregory wouldn't make the cut. The man seriously gave her the creeps. But his family did make huge contributions to the charity, so she'd choose her words wisely.

"I—"

"Ready to go?"

At Will's unexpected question, Natalie blinked at him. He joined them and placed his hand possessively on Natalie's back. His touch seared through her clothes, causing her to gulp. "Go where?"

"Whatever you feel like is fine. I've no real preference on where we dine this evening." Will's intense gaze connected with Gregory's, warning the other man to back away.

What was he doing? And even more importantly, why was he doing it? Surely he didn't think he had to protect her. But everything in the way he eyed the other man said that was exactly what he was doing.

"I ate prior to the meeting." Part of Natalie rebelled against his high-handedness. Another part was grateful he'd realized what was happening and was giving her an easy out to escape Gregory without offending and possibly causing detriment to the Children's Cancer Charity.

"But, if you don't mind waiting, I'll be ready to leave in a few minutes."

Will's green gaze not leaving Gregory's, he nodded. "I've never minded waiting on you, Natalie. When you're finished, I'll walk you home."

She'd swear his comment was directed at Gregory more than herself, reiterating that Natalie was off-limits. As Will had never shown jealousy in the past, had never had reason to, Natalie fought to keep her jaw from dropping. Had he really never minded waiting on her?

Insides shaking, she gathered up her notebook, then went to talk to Katrina and one of the parent volunteers. Only her gaze kept going back to where the two men still stood.

"I thought—" Gregory said loud enough anyone in the room could hear.

"You thought wrong," Will corrected, then in a voice that would have made Rebecca proud had Natalie not been the subject, he ordered, "Stay away from Natalie."

Will walked away from the red-faced man, going over to where Lee was chatting with a couple of the parent committee members. After a few minutes, the parents left them on their own.

Natalie's heart raced. She smiled at the right times as she chatted with her cochair and fellow committee member, but her mind was on the man talking to his medical school buddy. Their voices were too low for anyone to hear what they said, for which Natalie was both grateful and wished she could move close enough to overhear.

By the burning of her ears and the way Lee kept looking her way, she was the topic of conversation.

When Natalie had procrastinated as long as she could, she hugged her notebook to her like a shield and made her way to where Will and Lee laughed at something.

She'd thank him for saving her the trouble of dealing with Gregory, then head out on her own.

"Ready to go?" Will asked when she joined them.

Noting that Gregory was still in the meeting room and was watching them, she decided they could part ways on the street below. "Let me grab my bag."

Will said his farewell to Lee, as did Natalie after she'd gathered her things, then they headed toward the elevator bank. When the door slid open, there were already several people in the car, chatting away, saving Natalie from feeling as if she had to make conversation to avoid silence.

Once they stepped outside the building onto the still-busy sidewalk, Natalie prepped herself for saying goodbye. Polite. Professional. Grateful. She had this.

"Thank you for saving me from possibly having to make a scene in there. Gregory can be a bit much."

Will shrugged. "You're welcome. He's not someone you need to be alone with."

"I agree, and appreciate you giving me an easy out."

"No problem."

She hesitated, searching for the right words. "But I'd have handled it since it's really not your place to rescue me anymore."

His eyes glittered with the reflection of the streetlights.

"When we were a couple it was different," she clarified. "We're not now, so I need to, and can, handle things on my own."

"It's not a big deal, Natalie. I did what any gentleman would have done where Gregory is concerned."

Maybe. She didn't want to seem ungrateful, because he had simplified things. Under different circumstances it wouldn't have been a big deal. But this was Will and anything to do with him was a big deal.

Still, he was right. She was making a mountain out of a molehill over something he'd as much as said he'd have done to rescue any woman.

"Thank you, then," she said, then forced a polite smile. "I'll be on my way. There's no real need for you to walk me home."

His brow arched. "I said I would walk you home, so I'll walk you home, Natalie. Unless there's a reason you'd rather traipse the streets of Manhattan alone at night than be escorted by me?"

He made the route to Callie's sound dark and danger-ous. It wasn't. But, rather than argue, she bit the inside of her lower lip, welcoming the pain as it kept her from admitting that she didn't want him to walk her home be-cause putting Gregory in his place would have been easier than fighting her body's reaction to being near Will for the ten-plus blocks home. Knowing he was waiting for a response, she nodded then took off walking.

"Are you still at Callie's?"

"For the time being," she admitted, relieved that he'd changed the subject to something benign. "She and Brent have offered to let me have my old bedroom back per-manently, but I'm still of the mindset that I shouldn't en-croach on their newlywed time together. I'm scanning the roommate wanted ads daily in hopes of locating a place that works."

"It's a big city. Something should come up."

"You'd think," she agreed. "Finding something that's within a reasonable walking distance of the hospital and affordable seems to be almost impossible. I've given up and started looking at traveling back and forth by sub-way." Nervous, she kept talking. "I looked at a place earlier today, actually, that I thought was going to be perfect. But the ad was deceiving about the monthly rent and it ended up being way outside my budget."

Had the real monthly figures been put before her from the beginning she could have saved herself the trouble of viewing the place.

"Do you need money, Natalie?"

Confused, she looked his way. "For what?"

"An apartment of your own. The one you looked at today that you wanted, do you want me to arrange it for you? Say the word and I'll make it happen."

Were they back to that?

"No," she gasped, horrified that he'd thought she'd been hinting. "I'd never let you do that." She shook her head in denial, angry that he'd thought she would. "Besides, why would you be willing? We're no longer together. I'm not your responsibility, Will. Not where other men are concerned and not on where I live."

They paused at a street crossing and he took a deep breath. "In some ways I'm responsible for you not having a place to live."

The light changed and the waiting crowd started moving.

"Not really," she corrected, resuming walking in the direction of Callie's apartment. "You just delayed the inevitable. Callie and Brent had gotten engaged months prior to you asking me to move in with you. My moving out made their going ahead and marrying easy because they didn't have to worry about me and where I'd go. For that, I'm grateful because I wouldn't have wanted to stand in their way. So, I would have had to find another place and roommate, regardless of you and me."

Had the suspicion that Callie and Brent were delaying a trip to the justice of the peace because of Natalie living in the apartment played a role in her decision to move in with Will? She hadn't thought so, but she knew what she'd told him was true. Just as she knew it was true that she needed to find a place of her own and get out of their hair. But she'd stay put forever before she'd let Will set her up in an apartment.

They walked in silence for long enough that Natalie glanced his way, realized he was lost in deep thought.

"Whether you view me as responsible or not, I do feel responsible that currently you're essentially homeless. Give me the address of the place you looked at earlier. I'll set you up in it, help you get on your feet in your own place for however long you need. It's the least I can do."

She stopped walking and gawked at him.

"No," she said with enough force she hoped he got the message. "I wouldn't have allowed you to set me up in an apartment at any point in our relationship. I'm sure not willing to now. Listen to me carefully as I say this again, I'm not your responsibility and, in case you failed to notice, I never wanted your money."

His lips pursed and she could tell he was still plotting. "The money is nothing to me."

Exactly, she thought, and it was a big deal for her and most of the world.

"I don't need your money or your help."

She took off walking again, increasing her pace because she was ready for their walk to end. Well, part of her was. Another part was saying, *This is Will. Your Will. Walk slower so you can be near him longer.* Yeah, that part of her was crazy.

"I'll find the right place for me that's within my budget," she said, hoping to silence the voice in her head. "Until then, I'm fine at Callie's."

And hopefully she wasn't too much in the way. Her

friends were out on a date night to watch a new theater production. They'd invited her, but even if she hadn't had the gala meeting, no way would she have intruded on their date.

Focused on her thoughts, she stumbled, but didn't fall thanks to Will reaching out to steady her.

"You okay?"

All except where his hand burned into her flesh, melting her insides.

"Um…yeah, fine," she mumbled, not looking up at him. Could he tell how his touch affected her? That she hadn't wanted him to let go of her arm? That what she'd really have liked was him taking her hand into his and… No, she wouldn't have liked that. Their hand-holding days were long past.

Only…she snuck a glance his way and was struck by how handsome he was, by how safe she really had felt with him at her side during their walk. Her heart thundered so loudly in her chest he must have heard, because he turned toward her.

"Natalie?"

She swallowed. "Hmm?"

"Is everything okay?"

No. Nothing had been okay for months. Not from the point she'd started feeling as if he was hiding something from her. Was Stella's return to New York what had triggered his withdrawal from her? She'd not heard anything about him dating the blonde beauty, but she'd purposely avoided social media where photos might pop up of his after-work life.

"Just a long day," she answered, knowing he expected an answer and knowing she didn't want to tell him where her thoughts had gone. Her insides ached at what they'd once had and lost.

"Tired?"

She should be. She'd gotten up early, cleaned the apartment, then spent the biggest portion of her day volunteering with Katrina to prepare for the meeting. But looking into his green eyes, seeing something flickering there, as if he was asking something so much more than his single word, she just felt energized.

"No. I'm not."

"Because tonight's meeting went well?"

It had gone well, but she didn't credit that for the energy moving through her.

"I'm very proud of you, by the way."

Natalie missed her step but recovered without his help again. "For what?"

"For the amazing work you've done on getting the gala together and for how with each meeting you shine a little brighter. I recall how you weren't sure you were the right person for the job of cochair. I never doubted that you were."

Natalie looked toward him in a bit of awe.

"That shine was probably just me being embarrassed by one of my many blunders," she said, trying to damp down how good his praise made her feel. How hearing him say he was proud of her made her want to throw her arms around him and...

No, she couldn't do that. If her arms went around him, gratitude would soon morph into something so much more powerful.

"I doubt anyone noticed any mistakes you may have made," he assured, one corner of his mouth lifting.

"Except you?" she asked, knowing he'd been on to her when she'd said his name out loud. Had he also seen where she'd written his name? Known that he distracted her?

"I know you better than most, but like I said, I'm very proud of you. You're an amazing woman, Natalie."

Natalie couldn't hold back her smile. "Thank you. That means a lot to me."

Because he meant a lot to her.

"I think you're pretty amazing, too."

He smiled back and they walked the rest of the way to Callie's in silence.

When they arrived, Natalie paused outside the door. Unlike his apartment complex, there was no doorman, just a keypad code to get into the high-rise building.

"Thank you, Will. I really do appreciate your help with Gregory and for you walking me home."

He nodded. "You're welcome. I enjoyed stretching my legs and the company."

Natalie bit into her lower lip. "Callie and Brent are gone to a show."

Now, why had she told him that? She'd pretty much just hinted that she wanted him to come up. She didn't. Only…she did.

"Did you really already eat? We could go somewhere," he offered, his gaze searching hers.

"I did, but if you've not, then we could…" She paused. What was she doing?

"It's a long walk back to my car. Maybe just a glass of water before I head that way would be nice."

Realization dawned. "You drove to the meeting?"

His gaze locked with hers and he gave a wry grin. "I did."

"I'm confused. Why did you walk me here, then, knowing you'd have to make the walk back to get your car?"

"Because I said I would." He'd gone completely out of his way and had to backtrack now. Good grief. But she'd enjoyed their walk, too, and would forever treasure his having told her he was proud of her. "And, I wanted to walk with you, Natalie."

Natalie opened her mouth, then clamped it shut. What was she supposed to say to that? Feel at his admission? Because her insides had just gone into circuit overload.

"Fine. One drink of water, then you should be on your way before it gets any later."

But even as she punched in the keypad code that unlocked the double glass doors, Natalie's pulse raced, pounding in her ears. Thirst hadn't been what she'd seen in those brilliant green eyes. Which meant she shouldn't be letting him come upstairs and yet, she was.

Had she lost her mind? She needed to tell him she'd changed her mind, and if he needed water he could stop by a shop on his walk back. Only every nerve cell lit up and pulled her toward him as they waited for the elevator door to welcome them inside. And he was looking at her as if he knew her thighs were clenched beneath her skirt in response to the thought she was taking him up to Callie's apartment.

Callie's empty apartment.

Where they'd be alone.

Just the two of them. Her and the most beautiful man she'd ever set eyes on and who'd said he was proud of her. Did he have any idea how his words made her chest swell? How his smile had sent her stomach into cartwheels?

She was pretty sure she chattered some gibberish on the elevator ride up to Callie's floor, continued to blabber while she unlocked the apartment door, but for the life of her she had no clue what she said.

It must have been something amazing, though, because the moment they were inside the apartment and she turned to tell him she'd be right back with his water, he pulled her to him, and held her close, his eyes searching hers.

"It's not water I'm thirsty for, Natalie. You know it's not."

"I know," she admitted, heart racing, breath ragged, good sense nowhere to be found as her palms cupped his face and she stared up into the face she saw every time she closed her eyes and drifted into a dream world.

"I'm going to kiss you," he told her, his emerald gaze locked with hers and demanded she hide nothing from him. "If that's not what you want, tell me to leave now, because we both know a sip won't be enough to quench my need."

She knew what he was saying. Good Lord, she knew. They couldn't do that. They just couldn't. Not when they weren't together, and it wouldn't mean anything but just sex.

Only, this was Will and, on her part, being with him could never be just sex.

"Leave," she somehow managed to choke out. Then, as he immediately let go of her and took a step back, all her willpower drained. To her chagrin, she touched his arm. "No. Don't."

Rather than take her back in his arms, he studied her, waiting for her to say what she wanted him to do. If she told him to go, he would. Of that she had no doubt. He wouldn't seduce her and allow her to blame him for whatever happened between them. The choice was hers. All she had to do was say yes and he'd kiss her. Did kisses without love feel the same? Then again, she'd been the only one in love. If they had sex, to Will it would be nothing other than physical gratification. It's all it had ever been. Only, it had felt like so much more.

Natalie gulped back all the regret she knew she was going to have for what she was about to say, about to do. But Lord help her, this was Will and all she had to do was say the word and his lips would be against hers. How could she say no? No matter what tomorrow brought, she wasn't strong enough to deny herself the pleasure she knew he would give.

"I don't want you to go, Will," she admitted, somehow managing to keep her gaze locked with his.

His smile was lethal when he moved closer and his breath tempted her lips with his nearness. He was a man used to getting what he wanted and knew tonight was no exception. He wanted her and she was his. "You want me to kiss you?"

Or maybe *she* was getting what she wanted. Yet, *want* seemed such a tame word to describe the desire over-taking her.

"I need you to kiss me," she countered, knowing any semblance of pride was long gone. Will was here and for a brief moment in time, he'd be hers again. Logic told her that he wasn't, that he hadn't ever really been hers, but sanity was long gone. What was real was how her body sparked to life in anticipation of the magic he wielded. "Kiss me, Will. Please."

Her words snapped whatever held him back. With a growl from deep in his throat, his arms enveloped her, pulling her close, his hands molding her to him as his mouth covered hers in kiss after kiss.

Thirsty, he'd said. She felt it, too. Almost savagely so. Only, she wasn't sure who was devouring whom because she craved everything about him. His hands, his mouth, his body.

Against hers, his lips tasted sweet, triggering deep

aches. Aches that consumed her and grew hotter and hotter with each touch.

She hadn't meant for this to happen, that wasn't why she'd let him come up to the apartment. And yet, during that elevator ride hadn't she known exactly why Will was coming up with her? She shouldn't have put herself into that situation. But now that he was there, kissing her, she couldn't imagine not kissing him, not having her every breath filled with his. She'd never been able to resist this wonderful man who'd once filled her thoughts every waking moment. Who was she kidding? He still did.

She kissed him with the desperation of a woman who'd been deprived of oxygen and he was her air. She kissed him with the desperation of a woman who had loved and lost but was being given a short reprieve from her broken heart.

Which was why when he tugged her shirt from her skirt, she not only let him, she helped him and returned the favor, sliding her hands beneath the crisp material of his button-down.

Mine, she thought, as her palms skimmed over his abs and around to his muscled back. Mine. Mine. Mine. Only, he wasn't.

The thought that this might be the last time she ever touched him, kissed him, spurred her on, making her want to put every caress to memory, to imprint his taste upon her lips. She clasped his broad shoulders, holding on to him as tightly as she could as he shimmied her skirt up her thighs so he could cup her bottom.

"Will," she whispered, loving his name on her lips.

"Yes, my sweet Natalie," he replied, his fingers looping around the lace of her panties and sliding them down her legs to pool at her feet.

His eyes met hers, dark with desire, but with just

enough hesitancy that she knew he was making sure she was still with him before they went any further, that this was what she wanted.

Could he have any doubts? She couldn't imagine so as she lifted one foot, then the other, and stepped out of her underwear and nudged them away with her toes.

"Natalie," he moaned, but otherwise he didn't talk and for that she was grateful.

She didn't want words or reason. She wanted him. She felt as if she'd always wanted him. Maybe she had because he was the man of her dreams in so many ways.

Soon, she was pressed to the door, her skirt bunched at her waist, and her legs wrapped around his hips. His mouth feasted on her throat, her lips.

When he positioned himself against her, her breath caught and, gaze meeting his, she imagined everything she'd ever felt for him shone in her eyes. Part of her believed that's what she saw looking back at her in those beautiful green eyes of his, too. No doubt lust blurred her vision.

"Will," she gasped as, eyes still locked with hers, he thrust deep inside, claiming her and sending her body into spasms of pleasure. "I—I like that."

She'd almost said *I love you*. She'd stopped just in time, reminding herself that this wasn't about love, just physical chemistry.

If only she could believe that was completely true.

Will's breath ragged, he dropped his damp forehead against Natalie's and tried to make sense of what just happened. They were over so how had he ended up walking her home and taking what her sweet body so generously gave to his?

Of course he knew the answer.

There had always been something about Natalie that drew him to her in ways he'd never experienced, making him long to see her smile, hear her voice, give her pleasure.

He'd meant to kiss her, to slowly make love to her and pull orgasm after orgasm from her lush body. Instead, all power of reason had left him long before he'd pushed into her velvet. He'd been so in awe that he was touching her, kissing her, and that he got to feel her heat, there'd been no room for sanity. He'd looked into her eyes that were dazed with pleasure, lost himself in the big brown depths and just marveled that he once again held this special woman. His Natalie, who he'd missed so much.

And he'd rushed the whole thing.

"I shouldn't have done that," he murmured. He should have made love to her slowly, not taken her as if she meant nothing to him. They should have at least made it to the sofa rather than barely inside the door. She deserved better than that.

Natalie's eyes opened and filled with regret.

"Right," she murmured, wiggling free to stand on her own two feet. "You just wanted a glass of water and I... never mind. Sorry."

Will's stomach twisted at her instant tension. He didn't want to let her go but had no right to hold her to him, not when she wanted to be free, so he dropped his arms. Seeing the embarrassment in her cheeks, he cursed at his bumbling the moment yet again. "That's not what I meant, Natalie. You know that's not what I meant. What we just shared—"

"Was a mistake." Not looking at him, she smoothed her skirt down over her hips. "No worries. You just said what we both already knew. Neither of us should have done that. We have great physical chemistry, but we're wrong together."

Her words were burning arrows striking deep in his chest. When his gaze had been locked with hers, their bodies one, he'd have sworn nothing could be more right than Natalie being in his arms.

And not just because of physical chemistry.

"I wanted you but should have had more finesse than to take you against the living room door as if…" As if she weren't special, he finished in his head.

Natalie had always been different from any other woman he'd ever known. Not just because the sexual chemistry but because she made him feel more alive, more aware of every breath he took, more appreciative of his life's blessings. He'd not told her how much he appreciated her nearly as often as he should have. He'd not held her as tightly as he should have. He'd gotten so distracted by life and lost her.

"I wasn't complaining," she surprised him by saying with a bit of a whimsical smile that tugged at something deep within him and had him wanting to wrap his arms around her and hold on forever.

Which was a problem since she was no longer his. They'd had their shot and it hadn't worked. So why, even knowing that, did he suddenly wish they could start over? He wished he could scoop her up into his arms, carry her to wherever she was sleeping, and spend the night worshiping her body and convincing her that they were worth a second chance.

"I'd like to see you again, Natalie."

Her gaze cut to his. "You see me right now."

"True, but yet again you're purposely misunderstanding me."

She hesitated. "Then tell me, Will. When you say you want to see me again, what do you mean?"

She was looking at him, listening to him, giving credence to what he was saying, and it thrilled Will, made him think maybe they could figure out something for their future. Something where they could see each other and decipher exactly what it was they felt for the other. Somewhere where they could shut out the world and it could just be the two of them. Somewhere Natalie chose where she could be happy and feel comfortable. Somewhere they could laugh and smile together and see if the bonds they shared could be weaved into something unbreakable.

"Let me set you up in an apartment, Natalie," he urged, his mind racing ahead, wanting her to know he'd listen to her this time, that if she hadn't been happy in his home, they didn't have to stay there. "Just pick one, whatever makes you happy, and it's yours."

Which was apparently the completely wrong thing to say because her smile disappeared and she clammed up, moving away from him.

"No."

In frustration, Will ran his fingers through his hair. "What just happened between us—"

"What just happened between us shouldn't have happened," she interrupted as she looked around until she spotted her panties against a wall where she'd kicked them.

"I disagree," he said. "What just happened between us is what we do best."

"It's everything else we have issues with," she murmured, picking up her underwear.

He wanted to argue. They hadn't had issues with everything else. They'd been just fine until he'd messed up her birthday party and she'd walked away. At least, as far as he'd known, they'd been just fine. He'd thought their relationship solid. They could start over, take things slower this time, work through their issues—his mother, her insecurities, his not having appreciated her the way he should have and whatever else had driven them apart.

"We don't have to live together," he attempted to explain, doing up his pants. "You were right about that." Apparently, since living together had led to their no longer being together. "Let me help you."

Her gaze darkened to the point her chocolate eyes appeared black. "By setting me up in an apartment so you can stop by anytime you feel like a repeat of what just happened?"

Heat stung his cheeks. "It wouldn't be like that."

"That's exactly what it would be like and my answer is no. No. No. No!" Her tone grew angrier with each word and with the last she threw her underwear at his chest. "Go away, Will."

Frustrated, Will caught the scrap of lace and clenched it in his fist.

"I'm trying to help you, Natalie. I want to help you. Why are you making things more difficult on yourself than they have to be?" Why was he doing such a terrible job of conveying that he wanted to make things better for her, that there was no need for her to be crashing at Callie's when he would gladly help her get into a place of her own? A place where they could start over.

Her breath huffed out. "I'll move back to New Jersey with my parents and commute into the city every morning before saying yes to being your paid sex toy."

Will grimaced. Was that how she thought he viewed her? Yes, he'd gotten caught up in what they'd just done, but he cared about her, didn't want her struggling when making things easier for her would be so simple. "That's not what I'm asking you to do."

Rather than relax, her fists went to her hips and she glared at him as if she wished she could make him disappear forever. "You're saying you want to set me up in an apartment and that we wouldn't ever be having sex?"

"You still want me," he reminded, hurt that she was pushing him away yet again despite what they'd just done. She'd proven that her body craved his as much as his did hers, and she wouldn't have shared her body with him if she didn't still care.

"At no point have I said that I didn't want you," she immediately flung back, then marched over to snatch her underwear out of his hand.

Her answer had him pausing. She'd never stopped wanting him. He sure hadn't stopped wanting her. And yet they hadn't worked.

"But I sure don't like you very much at the moment," she told him as she stepped into her panties. "It's been a long day. I'm not very happy with myself at what just happened between us. I'd really prefer it if you leave now, Will."

CHAPTER FIVE

WHETHER OF HIS own accord, because of prior commit-
ments, or because of Will's warnings two evenings previously, Gregory was a no-show for the fundraiser meeting
Natalie arranged at the hospital on her next day off work.
She'd figured meeting at the hospital for a quick lunch
would be easiest on Will and Dr. Lewis and would be a
safe, neutral location.

After the way she'd practically thrown herself at Will,
inviting him up to Callie's apartment and embarrassing
herself, Natalie was completely mortified, and needed
safe and neutral. How could she have been so foolish as
to have sex with Will?

As usual, Dr. Lewis treated her with the kindness that
no doubt made him an excellent pediatric oncologist. The
man had heart.

Whereas the other man sitting at the table acted as if
he didn't want to be there but had felt obliged to attend.
That made two of them. She'd wondered if he wouldn't
show, but since the gala was important, he'd been right
on time. Natalie would do everything she could to make
it a success. Which was why she'd distracted herself most
of the previous day by researching corporate charities,
making lists and consulting with Katrina.

Mostly, she'd just been trying to avoid Callie and

Brent's apartment because every time she went through the apartment doorway, she had flashbacks. Plus, with her nerves so torn up, they must hate sharing a bathroom with her. Nothing wanted to stay in her stomach since prior to her birthday party. A broken heart could really work a number on a person. At least at the Children's Cancer Charity office, it was just her and Katrina there most of the time to share the bathroom.

"I made some calls after our meeting the other night. Several of my peers plan to purchase tickets to attend the gala, including their staff. Plus, they've committed to making donations." Lee gave a low laugh. "The board should be all smiles at this year's fundraiser and the amazing things we'll be able to accomplish with the funds raised." He nudged Will's shoulder. "Because I have faith that this guy's going to top everything I've done. Knowing him, he already has."

Natalie had been avoiding looking directly at Will, but at Lee's comment her gaze shifted to him. He'd not made eye contact with her, either, but kept glancing at his watch as if he had to be somewhere soon or was bored by the conversation. He was a busy heart surgeon and it was the middle of his workday. Of course he had other things he needed to be doing.

"I'll keep this short," she began, making sure he knew she didn't want to be there any more than he did. Seeing him only reminded her how weak she was where he was concerned. "I've done an online search of the companies we should qualify for. I've printed my list and their donation application process. Several aren't taking new charity applications currently, but for the ones that are, we need to apply. I also plan to send out a batch of email invites to the gala, again. Katrina is helping."

"Good idea," Lee praised, looking impressed. "Do we need to divvy up the application list?"

Natalie hesitated. She'd planned to ask them, but both men were busy doctors. She had the rest of the day off and could get most of the applications done if she worked on them. But when she realized that she was yet again valuing others' time more than her own, she nodded. She had to start placing value upon herself and her time.

"That would be great."

There, that wasn't so difficult.

"I met with Katrina this morning and we went through my list. I've printed a couple of the applications that, with her help, I've done as a guide to know the correct answers on the forms. Anything you need to know should be on one of the examples, but if you run into problems don't hesitate to reach out to myself or Katrina. I think it'll make going through the list much simpler as they all seem to need similar information."

They continued with the brief meeting until Lee's phone pinged. Glancing at his message, he frowned.

"Sorry, guys, but I've got to run." He grabbed the file folder Natalie had handed him. "I'll get this taken care of." He paused, then grinned. "To be fair, it'll likely be by one of my staff, but I'll make sure it's done within the next twenty-four hours."

When he was gone, Will opened his file to peruse the names on the list. When he'd skimmed over the top page, he lifted his gaze. "If that's everything, I've a busy schedule."

"That's everything." She went to pick up Greg's file folder, figuring she'd take care of his list after she did her own. Much simpler to do that than to reach out to the man and open herself up to having to interact with him.

"I'll take that." Will gestured to the folder she held.

"You want Gregory's list?"

He nodded. "I'll see that it gets addressed by myself, or my staff."

She gave him the file, feeling a bit guilty for doing so, then reminded herself that he'd probably hand it off to a staff member like Lee was planning to do.

Instead of immediately leaving, he flipped it open and scanned over the names on the list. "You gave Stella Fashion to Gregory?"

Natalie's face heated. Had she?

"Not intentionally," she defended, hating how she could feel the heat rising in her face. "I just randomly cut the list and placed them in the folders. She just happened to be in the folder that was left for Gregory."

"Right."

"You think I intentionally didn't give Stella to you?" She snorted, shaking her head at him. "Wrong. Had I given it any thought, I'd have purposely given her to you since you are such *close* friends. How could she say no if you ask her to donate?" She smiled sweetly. "Plus, now that Gregory's not here to do his part and you're taking his list, what does it matter? You have your excuse to contact Stella."

He glared at her. "I don't need an excuse."

Ouch. Natalie's heart tanked somewhere in the vicinity of her big toes. She swallowed. Was he purposely trying to make her jealous? If so, he was doing a good job, because the blood flowing through her arteries had turned as vividly green as his eyes. "You're seeing her, then?"

Oh, how she hated that she'd not been able to resist asking.

"She's Mother's goddaughter," he reminded her, "and had dinner with my family last evening."

Two nights ago he'd taken Natalie against the door.

Last night he'd had dinner with Stella. Had he...? No. She was not letting her mind go there. Not happening. What Will did was his business. Only...

She could feel him studying her, could feel how his gaze on her was speeding up her pulse.

Not quite meeting his eye, she tried to sound nonchalant as she said, "That's great."

Great for Stella. Or Rebecca. But for Natalie—yeah, not so much.

Not thrilled with himself for testing Natalie to see if she was jealous, Will watched as red splotched across Natalie's throat. He shouldn't have mentioned Stella. She meant nothing to him, and he hadn't been pleased to see her at his parents' the evening before. He'd thought he'd been called over for a quick dinner with them, and instead he'd walked into a setup. To say he'd not been happy with the arrangement was an understatement and he'd reminded his mother that relationship was dead and couldn't be revived.

Was that an accurate description of his relationship with Natalie? Perhaps their relationship couldn't be revived, but their feelings for each other weren't dead. Far from it. Not on his part and not on hers based upon the way her lower lip had just disappeared between her teeth and her pulse hammered at her throat.

"You don't have an issue with that, do you, Natalie?"

"Of course not."

What had he expected her to say? That she wanted him to remain faithful to her for all time?

If she'd wanted that, would he have been willing?

He started to ask, to admit he hadn't so much as thought of another woman that way since meeting her, but she spoke before he could.

"I've no right to have issues with whatever you do outside the hospital." She swallowed, then straightened her shoulders as if steadying herself for impact. "It's not as if I expected you to stay celibate when I moved out."

Memories hit of his being very much not celibate with Natalie just a few nights ago. They probably hit her, too, judging by her reddened cheeks.

"Just as you don't expect me to stay celibate," she continued.

Will couldn't prevent his sharp intake of breath or the heat that flooded his face as her words sank in.

"You've found an apartment, then?" he asked, trying to buy himself a moment to steady his nerves, and think of something to say that conveyed his sense of betrayal that she would allow someone else to touch her. Her comment had yet again caught him off guard to the reality that they were no longer a couple. "A place to start this new not-celibate life you want?"

He had no rights, yet the thought of her with someone else shredded his insides, causing his defenses to kick in and the voice inside his head to remind him that she'd left him, betrayed his trust and that some things were better left undone.

Her gaze didn't quite meet his as she shrugged. "Perhaps. I'm going to view another place this afternoon. A friend from nursing school called yesterday to say she was looking for a roommate and had heard I might be interested. We got along well together and have loosely kept in touch. It's a three-bedroom unit, so there's another roommate who I don't know, though. Hopefully, if everything is as I was told and, after seeing the apartment and if it seems a tolerable living situation, then I can get moved in soon."

Soon, so she could start her new life without him in it.

Panic hit. Natalie was moving on with her life and, despite whatever emotions lingered between them, she didn't want him in it.

Will's phone buzzed, causing him to glance at his watch. His lips tightened, then he picked up the file folders. His life was crazy enough without exposing his heart.

"I'll do as Lee promised and make sure these are addressed within twenty-four hours." His gaze met hers and, ignoring the tightening in his chest, he said, "Good luck on finding that tolerable living situation."

Natalie changed out an on-its-last-drops intravenous fluid bag for a fresh one, chatting to her nonresponsive patient as she did so. Jim Holland had been admitted for an acute cerebrovascular ischemic attack triggered by uncontrolled atrial fibrillation. While still in the emergency department he'd started having chest pain and when checked, his troponin levels had been elevated. He'd ended up in emergency cardiac surgery.

Will had put several stents in the man's heart, restoring blood flow to his ischemic myocardial tissue. But with the atrial fibrillation–induced stroke topped by the man's heart attack, the next twenty-four hours were crucial and, although his surgery had been a success, he'd suffered so much body trauma that no one was confident he'd pull through.

Both of Natalie's previous patients had been transferred out of the CVICU so it made logical sense that she'd been given Mr. Holland. Knowing she'd have to interact with Will before the end of the day made her heart heavy. Their interactions over the past two weeks since their lunch meeting had been professional, but terse. Hopefully, the intensive care unit's census would change soon so she would be needed there more than in the CVICU and she could go back to not having to see Will at the hospital.

Was there a procedure that healed a broken heart?

If so, sign her up. She'd had about all the moping, tears and nausea she could stand over the past few weeks. Every time she saw him was like a fresh wound into her already bleeding heart.

Glancing at her watch, she double-checked to make sure her patient was clean, then tucked his sheet in around him.

"Has he awakened?"

At Will's question, Natalie jumped. She'd been so lost in her thoughts, of him, that she hadn't heard him enter the room.

"I didn't mean to startle you."

"No problem," she assured. "No, he's not been awake since being transferred to my care."

"It's probably best for his recovery if he rests."

Natalie nodded. "It's almost time to let his family back for a few minutes. Do you want me to wait until after you've finished examining him?"

Will shook his head. "I met his wife earlier. Nice lady. Said they'd been married forty years and were high school sweethearts before that. She'll be anxious to see him."

Forty years. Natalie could only imagine the woman's anxiety at the day's events.

"If you don't need me, then I'll get her so she can spend a few minutes with him during visitation."

His mouth opened and for a moment she thought he was going to say something, but instead he turned his back to her, took out his stethoscope and placed the diaphragm against the man's chest without saying a word.

Natalie was still considering what Will had almost said when she returned to the CVICU room with their patient's wife. He was standing at the computer, logging in chart notes.

Rushing into the room, the woman took one look at her husband lying in the hospital bed with multiple tubes coming out of him and wires connected on various body parts and she crumpled. Natalie caught her, wrapping her arms around the woman, and trying to offer comfort where she could. In many ways, comforting family was the hardest part of her job.

"Mrs. Holland?" Will immediately came to her side. "We met earlier. I'm Dr. Forrest."

"I've met so many doctors today it's mostly a blur—" the woman blinked back tears "—but I do remember talking with you. You're the heart surgeon who operated on Jim."

Will nodded. "I know it's difficult seeing your husband this way, but he's fairly stable."

The woman's gaze bounced between Will and her husband.

"He's been through a lot today. It may be a few days before he wakes. I need you to be strong and encouraging because he may be aware of you being here despite his lack of consciousness."

The woman nodded as if she understood, but trembled against Natalie, who still held her, supporting a fair share of the woman's weight for fear she was going to topple.

"We'd been fighting earlier. I need to let him know how sorry I am for the things I said." The woman grimaced, then turned pleading eyes toward Will. "You think he knows I'm here?"

"Based upon how his blood pressure and heart rate sped up the moment you first spoke, I'd guarantee that on some level he's aware, and glad, you're here."

Natalie glanced at the monitor. Sure enough, the

man's heart rate had elevated from the baseline she'd previous recorded.

"As tempting as it may be, now isn't the time for rehashing your argument," Will advised gently. "Let him know you're here for him. Reassuring him that he's going to push through this is what's important and what he needs to hear."

Amidst her tears, Mrs. Holland nodded. "I... I can do that. I will do that."

And she did. Stepping away from where she leaned against Natalie, she took her husband's hand and stood by his bed. Between sucking back a few sobs, she began telling him how their children and grandchildren were in the waiting area and were so concerned. She told him how loved he was by his family and by her. She continued talking and his heart rate and blood pressure leveled off to a steady state.

"Come on," Will murmured, motioning to Natalie. "Let's give her a moment."

Realizing she'd been staring as if frozen in place, Natalie glanced toward Will, nodded, then touched the woman's arm. "I'll be right outside his room. If you need anything hit the call button or poke your head out."

Without looking away from her husband or pausing in the things she was saying to him, Mrs. Holland nodded.

They left the room, but Natalie hesitated outside the door as the woman yet again broke down in tears. When she started to go back into the room to offer any comfort she could, Will placed his hand on her arm.

"Don't. She needs a moment and we'll give it to her."

"Upsetting him isn't good," she replied.

"No, but I'm leaning toward his needing to hear what she's going to say. She's known him over forty years. My guess is she knows what words to say to make him want to fight to get well much better than we do."

What Natalie was hearing from his distressed wife was mostly "I love you," "I'm sorry," and "Please don't do this" over and over.

"Give her five to ten minutes and then ask her if she wants to swap out and let one of their children come back," Will ordered.

"Okay." But her attention was back on the room. "Will, she's sobbing uncontrollably. You're sure about this?"

"Give her a few minutes," he repeated, his voice firm. Part of Natalie knew he was right and loved the way he was so sensitive to the emotional needs of their patient's wife. Another part worried the woman's tears might upset her patient and left Natalie feeling protective as her number one job was his physical health and well-being. But she also believed in the power of a hug and if ever a person needed a hug, Mrs. Holland did.

She glanced toward Will and her breath caught at the light in his eyes. His gaze was filled with kindness as he watched the woman holding her husband's hand and murmuring words of love. Kindness and something more that almost looked like envy, but that couldn't be right.

With mixed feelings Natalie stepped away from the doorway, planning to sanitize then go check on her other patient for a few minutes as she was struggling with her desire to console Mrs. Holland. But mostly, she just wanted to escape being with Will because seeing that raw look in his eyes made her want to hug him, too.

His tenderheartedness and desire to do good by people was one of the many things that had made her fall for him to begin with. One of the many things she missed as she'd not seen that particular emotion in his eyes directed at her for some time.

Mostly, these days, she felt the same withdrawal in attitude toward her that he'd shown at their lunch meeting and every time their paths had crossed since. The only positive being it might help her get over him sooner.

Was getting over Will even possible?

"Nurse!" Mrs. Holland shrieked.

"Yes?" Natalie asked, rushing into the room.

"He squeezed my hand!" the excited woman gushed, practically jumping up and down as she clung to her husband's hand still. "Oh, my goodness, he squeezed my hand."

Relief washed over Natalie. Heart thundering as she'd feared her patient's condition was changing detrimentally, she squirted disinfectant on her hands. Then, along with Will, who'd also heard her cries and come rushing into the room, rechecked their patient.

"Whatever you said to him seems to have helped," Natalie admitted, pleased that the man flinched when she tested his pain response. He hadn't opened his eyes or said a word, but he was responding to certain stimuli and that was more than could be said prior to Mrs. Holland's arrival.

The woman gave a wobbly smile and lifted her husband's hand to her lips to press a kiss there. "I just told him how much he means to me, to our family. It's what a woman should tell a man every single day of her life because one never knows when that opportunity will be snatched away."

Why did the woman's words strike so deeply into Natalie's heart? She *had* told Will she loved him. Just once, but she'd told him, and what had he done? Pretended to be asleep. He sure hadn't ever said the words back. Then again, she wouldn't have wanted him to say words he didn't mean.

"Wise words," Will said from where he stood next to the hospital bed, smiling at the couple.

"True," Natalie agreed, fighting to keep her tone from revealing the turbulent emotions bubbling within her. "And it's just as true that a man should tell a woman how he feels about her every single day." Then her gaze shooting to Will, she arched a brow and added, "Or maybe a man telling her one single day would suffice if he said the right things."

"Natalie, girl, I don't know what you did, but you're amazing."

Dumping her bag and light jacket onto the small table where she worked in Katrina's office, Natalie glanced toward her committee cochair. Katrina's smile was so big it looked as if it was about to split her face.

"We've sold out of tickets!"

Stunned and thinking that was the best news she'd heard all day, Natalie exclaimed, "Really? Wow. That's wonderful."

"It really is except we're having to turn people away. I'm keeping a cancellation list, but just wow." Katrina clapped her hands together in glee.

"I guess the board will consider this year's gala a success, after all," Natalie mused. At least, she'd accomplished something positive over the past few weeks.

Katrina grinned. "Are you kidding me? They may offer you a seat on the board after this."

"Because we sold out of tickets?" Natalie asked, confused, sitting down in the chair in front of her makeshift desk. "I seriously doubt that."

Katrina looked as if she were about to burst with excitement. "Okay, so probably not on the board seat offer, but a lifelong position on the committee. Selling out of tickets is wonderful, but it's the corporate donations pouring in that will tip the scale."

"You've heard back from some of the applications, then?" Natalie had assumed it would be a lengthy process and might take months, long after the gala, before they'd hear anything back. "That really is wonderful. I wondered if any would respond before the gala."

"Heard back and received the check from a couple of big ones."

That news was almost enough to dissipate her perpetually sour stomach.

"Oh, wow. That is wonderful."

"What's wonderful is the amounts Harroway Industries, the Harroway Foundation, and Stella Fashions contributed alone." Katrina named sums that would take Natalie years to earn. "Girl," she continued, looking impressed, "it's good to be friends with that family."

That Katrina lumped Stella in as part of the Forrest family knotted Natalie's stomach. She wanted to correct her cochair but didn't. She just smiled and told herself that it didn't matter. Will had implied that he and Stella were dating. Who knew? Maybe Rebecca would get her way and Stella would be family soon enough.

A knife jabbed her heart at the thought, but she kept a fake smile on her face.

It did surprise her that Harroway Industries had made a sizable donation since Rebecca would be aware that Natalie was cochairing the committee. It also surprised her that Katrina had insinuated that she was friends with the Forrests. Because of the awkwardness of their last meeting, she'd told her cochair about her relationship status change.

Natalie turned to pull her laptop from her bag, but at her movement an intense wave of sickness hit.

"Excuse me," she said, rushing to the bathroom to lose the crackers she'd eaten that morning. Eventually her nerves had to level out. If not, she was going to shrivel away because nothing tasted good and what she did manage to force down didn't want to stay down. It was going on two months since her birthday. Maybe she needed to arrange for counseling.

"You okay?" Katrina asked when Natalie returned to the woman's office and sat back down.

Natalie gave the woman an apologetic look. "Not really, but I'll eventually get there."

Katrina continued to stare with concern. "Your face went ghost white and you high-tailed it out of here."

"Just nerves getting the best of me," she admitted, hating the fact that her friend had noticed she wasn't feeling well. "Again. Between the breakup, working extra shifts, working on the gala and planning to move into my new apartment the day after the gala, I've a lot going on."

"That is a lot." Giving her an empathetic look, Katrina nodded, then laughed lightly. "Just so long as you're not pregnant, eh?"

Pregnant? Natalie's head spun to where she wondered if she might fall out of her chair.

She couldn't be pregnant.

She was on a twelve-week cycle low-dose oral birth control pill and hadn't missed any. Not even after she'd moved out of Will's apartment and no longer thought she'd have a need for birth control. She wasn't due her menstrual cycle for another week. She'd not even considered the possibility as a cause of her persistent upset stomach because she'd protected herself from pregnancy.

But medications weren't foolproof.

For the rest of the afternoon, her mind kept straying to Katrina's comment. What if that was why she'd been so emotional? So nauseated and ill at her stomach? What if pending motherhood had played a role in why she'd no longer been willing to let herself be on unequal footing with Will and had wanted to be included in his family life? Of why, instinctively, she'd known she had to try to make things right between them because their baby was growing inside her.

Feeling ridiculous and very self-conscious, she stopped by a discount drugstore on her walk home and purchased a pregnancy test.

It would be negative. She wasn't pregnant.

Only, when she got back to Callie's and ran the test, two blue lines appeared.

Two blue lines!

She sank to the floor, leaning against the bathroom cabinet, and stared in disbelief at the test.

She was pregnant.

CHAPTER SIX

"You HAVE TO tell Will," Callie insisted over dinner that night. Brent was pulling an extra shift at the hospital as one of the respiratory therapists had called out ill and Natalie was grateful for the alone time with her best friend. If ever she'd needed advice, it was now.

"Of course I'll tell Will. It wouldn't be right not to." Picking at her Alfredo noodles, Natalie winced. "I mean, if it's real, that is."

"Real?" Fork halfway to her mouth, Callie paused. "Why wouldn't it be real? You showed me the test. There's two lines, Natalie. Two. As in, you're pregnant."

"It could be wrong," she said. "I might not be pregnant. It was just a simple drugstore test."

"Which are pretty doggone accurate," Callie argued, then ate a bite of her pasta. "That second line doesn't just magically appear. Human growth hormone has to be present to trigger a positive result."

Natalie set her fork down on her plate. "Yes, but it could be a false positive." Rare, she knew. "I can't go to Will and announce I'm pregnant if I'm not really." Just the thought of doing so and then discovering she wasn't made her stomach heave. "Can you imagine how horrific that would be? He'd think I was trying to trap him into a relationship."

"I get that," Callie relented, wincing at the thought. "I'd like to think he knows you better than that, though, but just to be sure, let's go get another test."

Natalie was already sorry that she hadn't bought every test in the store just to make sure there was no doubt on the results, so she nodded.

"We could pick one up," or two or three or however many they had for sale, "and I'll do it first thing in the morning. That's supposed to be the most accurate time."

Callie clasped her hands together. "Perfect. We'll go as soon as we finish eating."

Natalie nodded. "If it's positive, then I'll call for an appointment with my ob-gyn and take the first available appointment. If she says I'm pregnant, then, and only then, after I definitely know, I'll tell Will."

If.

What if she was?

What if she wasn't?

Because as scary as she found the prospect of pregnancy, as untimely as it would be to have a baby, the idea that Will's child grew inside her brought along an excitement. An excitement so strong that she knew she'd be disappointed if the additional tests were negative or her gynecologist said the home tests had been wrong.

Before she'd first noticed Will withdrawing from her, she'd have been ecstatic to learn she was pregnant. Now, when their relationship was over, a baby would make things that much more complicated.

"Hello." Callie snapped her fingers in front of Natalie's face. "If you are pregnant, your baby would be the heir to the Harroway fortune. That's a big deal."

What would Will say if she was going to have his baby? Would he think she'd gotten pregnant on purpose? Would he believe all the things his mother had insinuated about her? That she was nothing more than a gold digger looking to latch on to the Harroway fortune?

"I don't want money from Will's family. I have a great job and make a decent living. I've saved my money while living with Will. I can take care of this baby."

Callie frowned. "Will would insist on taking care of you and his child. You know he would. He's too decent not to insist."

Natalie's hand dropped to her lower abdomen. "First, there's probably not a baby. Second, if there is, Will has never said anything about wanting children. Third, if he does want to be a part of this baby's life—" and she agreed with Callie that he would because he was a good man "—I'll encourage him for our child's sake, but I won't take money from him."

No way would she allow Rebecca to use that against her. No doubt Will's mother would accuse her of intentionally getting pregnant to try to hang on to her son. On more than one occasion she'd implied Natalie was nothing more than a gold digger. Ha. Rebecca might not have worried quite so much if only she'd realized Natalie had spent most of her time wishing Will had been ordinary and not mega-wealthy.

"Most likely, I'm not pregnant and all of this is for nothing," she spoke the words out loud for her own benefit as much as to say them to her best friend.

Callie's eyes held sympathy. "You don't really believe that, do you?"

The test had been positive. False negatives were much more common, but the test could have been wrong. The likelihood was slim, though.

Natalie closed her eyes. "I don't know what to believe anymore. My brain and emotions have been every which way for weeks. At least, being pregnant would explain that and my almost constant nausea."

Her friend leaned across the table to rub her shoulder. "Well, know that Brent and I are here for you. You are welcome to stay indefinitely if the new apartment doesn't work out."

Natalie gave a small derisive smile. "You think my new roommates are going to kick me to the curb if I'm a package deal?"

"Who knows?" She shrugged. "Regardless, we're here for you." Callie pointed at her barely touched food. "Now, eat something because you may be eating for two and if you hurry we can walk to the drugstore around the corner to buy another pregnancy test so I can know for sure whether or not I'm going to be an honorary aunt."

Natalie wasn't hungry, but the possibility that there was a tiny life within her needing nourishment prompted her to pick up her fork and take a bite.

If she was pregnant, she'd do everything within her power to make sure she and Will had a healthy baby.

The following morning, the CVICU was slammed and Natalie had been at a run all morning. For the first time, she didn't mind her nausea so much, though. Not if Will's baby was why she felt so bleh.

Her second test had been positive. And so had the third.

What were the odds of three tests taken on two different days being false positives? Low. Very low.

She'd been giddy when the second line had appeared almost immediately on the second test. Giddy and so light-headed she'd thought she might faint. She was going to have Will's baby. Her best guess was that she was somewhere around eleven weeks pregnant as her menstrual cycle had been normal between her twelve-week pill packs. How would Will react to their news? They weren't together anymore. She couldn't imagine that he'd be nearly as excited as Natalie was.

Funny, she'd not known she wanted a baby, to start a family of her own, but she now craved it. If this was how her mother had felt, no wonder Natalie had such a big family.

"Have you called your gynecologist yet? She is an obstetrician, too, right?" Callie whispered when they met up at the medication cart.

"Yes, and not yet," she admitted. She'd hoped to sneak away long enough for a five-minute bathroom break and make the call in private to avoid being overheard. With the flurry of activity on the unit, she hadn't been able to slip away.

"Go, call now," Callie insisted, smiling. "I'll watch your patients."

Natalie laughed. "What's your rush?"

Callie's grin widened. "I want to be able to tell the world I'm going to be an auntie."

"Shh!" Natalie shushed her, glancing around to make sure no one was within hearing range. No one was. Thank goodness. "Don't say things like that."

She was excited, but not ready to share her news with anyone other than her best friend.

"Sorry." Callie gave a sheepish look. "I shouldn't have said that here, I know, but I don't know how you can stand it. It's not even me and I want to scream it to the world."

Natalie did want to scream it to the world. She was pregnant. It was surreal. But part of her wanted to keep it quiet for a bit longer, too. She needed a little more time to get used to the idea herself before dealing with others' reactions. Admitting that she was pregnant with William

Harroway Forrest's baby came with a lot of fallout. Plus, the risk of miscarriage during the first trimester was high, especially with as stressed as she'd been,

"If I really am—" and, Lord, she was going to be devastated if she wasn't after a night of dreaming of having a baby and three positive home tests "—then we'll have plenty of time to celebrate." Natalie's gaze went to her best friend's, then she smiled softly again. "It's not something I'd given much thought to before yesterday. Just one of those things I expected to do someday. But now, I'll be disappointed if I'm not."

Callie gave a nod, then grabbing her meds, sighed. "Let me go administer these, and then hopefully, things will be settled down here to where you can sneak away long enough to make that phone call."

"Hopefully."

But Natalie was still at a run when Will arrived to do his rounds. He wore hospital issue scrubs so had probably been in the operating room that morning or would be heading there soon.

Seeing him took her breath away and made her want to leap into his arms and tell him their news. They were going to be parents.

Would her baby have his distinct Harroway green eyes or her brown ones? His dark hair or her red? Would Will insist upon using his family names if their baby was a boy? If he wanted another William, would they call him Billy or Liam or... Good grief. She needed to stop immediately. She shouldn't be picking out names.

"You okay?" he asked, making her realize she'd just been standing there gawking at him, analyzing his features and wondering which ones their baby would inherit. All of them, she hoped. She wanted their child to look just like him.

"Fine. Never better," she responded. She took a deep breath and told herself to calm down, which wasn't easy to do when seeing him made her want to burst with joy and tell him she thought they were going to be parents.

Just because she was overcome with joy didn't mean he would be. They weren't together. Even when they had been, he'd never told her that he loved her or wanted to spend his life with her. Once upon a time, she'd believed he did, but she'd been wrong.

He studied her, then said, "There's a sparkle in your eyes today."

She wasn't surprised she was glowing. She felt as if her very soul shined brighter than the sun.

"Life is good. I've found an apartment," she said, thinking he might be expecting an explanation for her smiley disposition. She'd tell him everything soon, but not at the hospital, and not until she'd seen her doctor for confirmation. "You know I love Cal and Brent. But it will be nice to have my own space again."

Her own space where she'd need to figure out where she'd set up a crib and put all the baby things she'd need in her bedroom so she wouldn't encroach on the shared living space with her new roommates. Her gaze met his and she couldn't hold back her happiness. *Oh, Will, we're going to have a baby.* No matter what had happened between them, what might happen in the future, he'd given her a precious gift, and she'd forever be grateful.

"Life is wonderful, actually. How about you?"

His brows formed a V, revealing his confusion. No wonder. She'd been trying to protect herself by avoiding him. She'd likely been walking around zombified from her aching heart.

For a moment she thought he wasn't going to answer, but then, he said, "Same. Fine. Never better."

His apartment was so close to Central Park. Would he take their child for long walks or to visit the zoo or— Looking at him, she knew he'd be a good dad. She'd seen how he interacted with the kids involved with the Children's Cancer Charity Gala, his patience and tender heart. Which reminded her...

"Thank you for the donation for the Children's Cancer Charity. Katrina told me what you did."

He shrugged as if it was no big deal that his efforts had raised the event's coffers by tens of thousands of dollars. "No problem. It's a great organization and I like kids."

There went her heart doing cartwheels.

"That's good. I've never heard you mention that before."

Staring at her oddly, and no wonder, his gaze narrowed. "You're chatty this morning. What's gotten into you?"

Your baby. Maybe. Probably. Three positive tests likely.

"I—nothing. Just making conversation."

Rather than comment, he sighed, then, looking uncharacteristically tired, he glanced down the hallway. "I'm booked in the OR again within the hour and need to check on my patients. Which room is Kevin Conaway in?"

Which told her he was done with their personal conversation and that the only interaction he wanted to have with her was on a professional level.

"Four. About the time I got Mrs. Johnson discharged— she was looking great, by the way—the operating room called to request a room. It's been nonstop all morning, as I guess you are aware."

Still giving her a confused look, he asked, "Any changes since Mr. Conaway arrived on the unit?"

"None." She'd gotten the sixty-one-year-old settled and he'd been resting comfortably when she'd left his room fifteen minutes before. His telemetry had remained stable. "His output has been minimal, but otherwise is as expected."

"His history is that he has pneumonia and went into renal failure with his respiratory distress," Will supplied, although Natalie was already aware of that from taking the report at the man's transfer to the unit. "When everything started shutting down, his heart couldn't take it and stopped. His son was able to do CPR until the paramedics arrived to take over. They got him here just in time."

"I'd heard his son saved his life but wasn't sure what the details were," she said, pleased that Will was at least making a little extra conversation with her even if it was work related.

"Lives alone with his adult son. Has been fighting a virus for a couple of weeks. Got a lot worse during the night and ended up here," Will said as they walked toward the room, pausing to disinfect and glove up. "I'm still not convinced he'll make it through the day and if he does that he won't have brain damage from how long he was hypoxic, but I did everything I could to save him. Only time will tell if it worked and to what extent."

All of their patients in CVICU were critical. Unfortunately, some of them not making it was something Natalie dealt with too often as it was the nature of working with such ill patients.

"You're a good doctor and man, Will." The praise slipped from her lips unbidden.

He paused outside Kevin's room. "Where did that come from?"

Natalie's cheeks heated. Ugh. What was wrong with her? She shook her head as if to clear it and replied,

"Sorry. Guess you're right—I am chatty this morning because that just popped into my head and out my mouth."

Donning his gloves and a mask, he glanced her way, curiosity shining in his eyes. "For whatever it's worth, I've always thought you an excellent nurse as well, Natalie. Seems professionally, we respect and admire each other. Too bad personally that doesn't hold true and we failed."

Stunned at both his compliment and his assessment of their relationship, she watched him go into the CVICU room to examine his patient. They had failed.

Both of them.

Because as much as she blamed him for the things that had led up to her moving out, she also shouldered that blame. Had pregnancy hormones clouded her mind and made her so moody she'd reacted in ways she typically wouldn't have?

She had been overemotional.

She shouldn't have moved out. She should have stayed and fought for what she wanted—for Will—rather than letting his mother's digs get to her. She'd thought she was taking a stand, protecting her pride, but instead she'd made matters worse.

She'd been sleeping in the love of her life's bed, and she'd left because his mother's disapproval had made her question everything. Mostly, her own self-worth in deserving a place in Will's life. He'd never said he loved her, but he had cared about her and invited her to share his home. She should have talked to him, told him how she felt, shared her fears and insecurities. Regardless of how he'd reacted, she should have told him she loved him more than just the one time.

Because she did love him. Always had. Always would. Staring into the room, Natalie's heart swelled, and she couldn't resist placing her hand over her belly. She'd made so many mistakes. They both had, but Lord willing, somehow, she'd make her wrongs right, become the confident woman he'd once fallen for before she'd let his world chip away at her self-worth.

She wanted Will. She always had. But she'd believed the act of leaving would somehow let him know what she wanted, what she needed. How foolish.

She'd use everything within her power to win him back.

Everything except the baby inside her.

Because if Will only returned to her after learning of the baby, then she'd always doubt his love for her and would spend the rest of her life feeling unworthy, and as much as she wanted Will, she wasn't willing to be second best.

Which meant she had to figure out how to win him back and soon before her pregnancy started showing.

Currently, though, she needed to check her patient with him.

Why was Natalie standing in the doorway watching him as if Will was doing something out of the ordinary? And what was up with her compliment? Where had that come from?

Had it been such a rough day with his mother going into surgery this morning that his brain was playing tricks on him?

Regardless, Natalie snapped out of whatever spell she was under, came into the room, checked the man's catheter bag and grimaced. "He's still not having any significant urine output."

"Get a basic metabolic profile on him. Let's make sure his glomerular filtration rate hasn't dropped further.

Consult Nephrology, as well. We'll get them on board in case he needs dialysis. I was hoping things would turn around once he was out of surgery, but apparently not."

Natalie nodded, watching as Will did a bedside ultrasound of the man's kidneys. It wasn't his specialty, but he knew the basics and wanted to make sure blood flow or obstruction to the organs wasn't an issue.

Will winced at what he saw on the screen.

"What's that?" Natalie asked, staring at the image on the monitor.

"Good question." Because Will wasn't positive what the mass on the man's left kidney was. "Possibly just an incidental finding, but he needs a CT of his abdomen and pelvis." He moved the transducer around, trying to get measurements on the mass. "I suspect his creatinine is still too high to risk contrast, so we'll make do without."

Natalie nodded, still staring at the screen. "Is it on the adrenal gland?"

"Appears to be just behind it but may be invasive of both the adrenal and his kidney," he answered. "Guess we'll know for sure after the CT."

"Poor guy can't get a break," Natalie mused as she ungloved, then punched orders into the computer while Will continued examining their patient.

Apart from how talkative she'd been, something was different about the way Natalie was looking at him. He'd swear he saw some of the old adoration on her face. Only, he didn't understand what had put it back there. Nor had he ever understood what had caused it to vanish to begin with.

That wasn't completely true, he admitted, wiping the conducting gel off the transducer. Her unfounded issues with his mother and his regrettable dance with Stella seemed to have triggered the avalanche that had buried their relationship. He didn't buy that his and his mother's generous donations to the Children's Cancer Charity had been enough to put the light back.

When she finished typing in the order, she turned to find him watching, and smiled. Smiled.

Confused, pulse pounding, he kept his gaze locked with hers. "Call me after Nephrology has checked him or any of his results are back."

"Will?" she asked just as he reached the doorway, causing him to turn around. "Would you want to go to dinner tonight after my shift ends?"

Something had definitely changed. He could see it in her eyes. Those big browns were filled with hope he'd say yes.

Will's throat tightened. "I can't."

"Oh." Her face flamed red and that light in her eyes dimmed. "I... Okay."

"I can't," he began, knowing he would be at his mother's bedside once she was out of surgery and no matter how curious he was about the reason behind Natalie's dinner invitation, he couldn't go.

"No problem. I understand." But her expression said she regretted asking and was more than a little mortified that she had.

That dejected look got to him. It shouldn't have since she'd sure rejected him often enough over the past few weeks. But he couldn't stand how she'd bitten into her lower lip and appeared ready to disappear. He had always been astounded that someone so amazing could ever doubt herself and it left him wanting to protect her from the world.

God help him at how this woman got to him.

"I already have plans, Natalie," he admitted, wondering why he was still making excuses. She'd left him.

He didn't owe her any explanations. Whatever had her reaching out to him didn't matter. At least, it shouldn't matter. Though, judging by how his heart raced, it did.

She nodded as if she understood, but he could tell she didn't and was slipping back into the defensive shell she'd been hiding behind for weeks.

Let her go, he told himself. Even if she wanted to go to dinner for all the right reasons, how could he ever trust in their relationship without wondering if she'd change her mind and leave again?

He couldn't.

Realizing he'd been holding his breath, Will exhaled and watched Natalie go to the nurses' station, say something to Callie, then disappear.

His heart squeezed. Although she'd refused to admit she was worried, he'd seen the fear in his mother's eyes that morning when he'd checked on her one last time before being wheeled back to surgery.

Although the contract had been signed the day before and was in the lawyers' hands, the stubborn woman still refused to risk anyone at Harroway Industries finding out she was having health issues, so she was claiming to be on a business trip. She had been admitted under an alias and was paying cash for all her medical care to keep it from showing on her company insurance. She had also ordered his father to stay away, as a senator being at the hospital would draw too much attention.

God, he prayed everything went according to plan, and that the doctor didn't find anything unexpected, and that his mother was soon back at the helm of her beloved company.

It was best that things had ended with Natalie.

If his mother's pathology report from her procedure today came back showing her cancer had spread into the lymph nodes, she would be needing him more than ever.

CHAPTER SEVEN

How stupid was she? Natalie wondered. Had she really expected Will to jump for joy and say yes?

If only it were that simple.

But if she gave up at the first stumbling block, that didn't say much, either, did it? Wasn't that what she'd done in many ways when she'd left her birthday party?

No more. This was her future, her unborn child's future, at stake. Was she really just going to bow out again so easily?

Was she going to tuck her tail between her legs and let him spend the evening with another woman? If so, then she deserved to have lost him.

Sucking in a deep breath, she caught Will just as he was coming out of Kevin's room. Mustering up every bit of resolve within her, she pasted on what she hoped was a dazzling smile. "Is there anything I can say to convince you to change your plans tonight? To spend your evening w-with me instead?"

He grimaced and she knew there wasn't.

Oh, God. She'd asked Will to dinner and he'd grimaced. Had he just been being nice earlier when he'd said he already had plans?

Fine. What was a little wounded pride in the grand scheme of life? If she wanted Will—and hadn't she always?—then she was going to have to step outside her comfort zone.

Lifting her chin, she asked, "If not tonight, what about tomorrow night? I'll be here until end of shift, again, but could we go somewhere afterward?"

His gaze softened and her heart swelled. Maybe, just maybe, he was going to say yes.

"Things are complicated right now. I'm not sure what tomorrow is going to be like. It would be better if I say no, Natalie," he said instead, his tone gentle, as if he believed what he said, but didn't want to hurt her.

"Better for who?" Because she needed to know if it was already too late.

"Both of us." He sighed, stuck his stethoscope into his scrub pocket. "Everything I've said to you is true. I wasn't ready for us to end, but perhaps, in some ways, it's made things less complicated."

Less complicated? Ha. She was pregnant. How was that for complicated?

"I thought we had something special," he continued, his expression wistful. "I thought you felt the same, that, for the most part, you were happy." His eyes darkened to a deep green. "I know I was busy those last few weeks, but there were things going on." Glancing down the hallway as if he couldn't look at her a moment longer, he said, "The reality is, I need to focus on my family and work."

Telling him that his family was likely about to expand was on the tip of her tongue, but she couldn't do it.

If she and Will had any hope for the future, they needed to work things out before he knew about her pregnancy. Otherwise, no matter what happened or what he said, she'd never fully feel wanted. Since her self-doubts had played so much into her leaving, she couldn't risk telling him yet. If they were to work things out between them, it had to be because they both wanted their relationship to work, because they were both willing to put in the effort to make things good between them.

"Okay." Not that it was, but she smiled at him, hoping her uncertainty didn't shine in her eyes. "I'd hoped to talk to you about how the past few weeks have put things into perspective for me, too. Maybe if you have—" Her CVICU nurse manager stepped out of her office, catching Natalie's eye and frowning when she saw Natalie so close to Will. No doubt anyone looking their way could see that their conversation had nothing to do with patient care. Heat flushed Natalie's skin. She couldn't afford to lose her job. She needed it now more than ever. "Thanks for the update on Mr. Conaway," she said briskly. "I'll let you know the moment his CT scan results are available for your review. Have a good day, Dr. Forrest."

"Natalie?"

She paused but didn't turn to look back at him. If she did he might see the tears stinging her eyes. Tears she had no one to blame for except herself. Why had she wanted everything? Wanted him to love her and his family to accept her? Why couldn't she have been content with what she'd had? She'd had so much more than so many women ever experienced. Obviously, she had mush for brains. Only...

"You're an amazing woman. I'm sorry things didn't work between us." His soft words rammed a dagger through her chest, hitting its unintended target.

"Me, too," she replied because she truly was sorry, then took off toward her other patient's room as fast as she could go without appearing to be running away.

Once there, she drew the curtain, for once thankful her patient was unconscious. Then forcing herself to keep her tears silent, she gave in to them.

* * *

Natalie's words haunted Will, playing heavily on his mind, while he sat in his mother's hospital room. Natalie had looked so…different. She'd practically glowed when she'd asked him to dinner.

And had quickly dulled when he'd declined.

He hated that he'd caused that transformation, but what had she expected? That he would drop everything because she'd decided she wanted to go to dinner with him?

If not for his mother, he would have.

"William Harroway Forrest, have you heard a word I've said?"

Will blinked at his mother. Busted. She might have had surgery that morning, and still look frail with her monitors and lines, but she wasn't beyond calling him out.

"Sorry, Mother." He reached over and placed his hand over hers, not surprised when she ran her finger over the signet ring that had once been her father's and that she'd given to Will on his twenty-first birthday. "Can I get you anything?"

Resting against her pillow, she eyed him, then harrumphed. "The only thing I want you've already said I was banned from for the rest of the day."

He gave a wry smile. "You're right. No laptop. I promised your surgeon I wouldn't let you work for at least twenty-four hours."

He suspected that for all her huffing and puffing, she didn't really feel like working, anyway. Her normally vibrant skin was pallid, her eyes tired and a bit hazy from medications, and she'd been in and out of consciousness, mostly sleeping, since returning from the surgical recovery area to her private room. She grimaced with the slightest movement but hadn't uttered a word of complaint about her pain or loss of her breast—only showing frustration that everyone refused to let her work.

"Seems odd he's the one issuing all the orders when I'm the one footing the bill," she mumbled, then drowsily smiled as she curled her fingers around the tips of his. "Now, tell me that our Stella is what has you so distracted."

Stella? He frowned. He'd already told her that he didn't feel that way about Stella and their parting ways had been the right thing. Was she so medicated she'd forgotten?

"It was so good of her to drive me here this morning," she mused. Something Will had offered to do, but she'd insisted Stella would take care of. "I'm just so tickled she's back in your life."

Not wanting to upset her so quickly post-op when she already looked weak, Will considered letting her comment ride. Then again, maybe while she was trapped in a bed and had to listen would be the best time for him to reiterate what he'd been telling her for months.

"Stella isn't a distraction for me, Mother. I'm not sure she ever was. There's never going to be a romantic relationship between us again. It was a mistake the first time and a second time would just be tragic."

"Don't be so hasty, Will." His mother tsked. "Stella is a lovely girl who's bright, has a promising business and is from a good family. And she's my goddaughter, which is an added bonus."

"Not interested." Will was 99 percent positive Stella was no more interested in him than he was her. She did, however, adore his mother, and always had.

His mother sighed. "You need to get over the fact that she left. It was the right thing for her to do at the time."

Will's gaze cut to hers. "Stella or Natalie?"

They'd both left him. One had done him a favor by

doing so. The other…if she'd been destined to leave, then she'd done him a favor by not delaying further, too.

Surprise darkened his mother's eyes that were so similar to his own. "Why on earth would you think I meant Natalie or that you would want to get back together with her? You've nothing in common and it was obvious she didn't fit into our world."

Surprised, Will stared at his mother. "I'm not sure what you mean by 'our world,' but Natalie fit into my world. I liked her being in my world." He missed her being in his world. "I thought you liked Natalie."

Slowly lifting her hand, she brushed a short strand of hair back behind her ear. Will recognized the action as one she did when giving herself time to consider her response to something she found unpleasant. He'd never seen her use the gesture on him and supposed her medication dulled her senses. Interesting.

"Natalie was a nice enough girl, smart, pretty, and no doubt about it, you were the best thing to ever happen to her, but she was too different for your relationship to have worked out long term. She was just standing in the way of you finding real happiness."

It was only natural his mother would think the best of him. He was her only child. But hearing her assessment of his relationship with Natalie hit him hard. It had to be her post-surgery pain medications loosening her tongue, but negativity seeped into her tone and left an uneasy feeling in his stomach.

"I'm curious as to why you think I was the best thing that ever happened to Natalie?"

His mother was rarely caught off guard, and perhaps it was only the remnants of anesthesia and heavy doses of pain medication, but clearly his question surprised her. "Because you're you and she's…"

"An amazing woman who's an excellent nurse and a blessing to every patient in her care? A beautiful soul who put me and others before herself time and again?"

"Oh, God." His mother's gaze narrowed. "You fancied yourself in love with her, didn't you?"

Had he? Will shook his head. Natalie had said the words to him once. He'd been so caught off guard, so humbled and yet so exposed, that he'd pretended to be asleep rather than deal with his reaction. Her words had swelled his chest with pride that such a woman could care so much for him.

Which was why he'd been so devastated when she'd left him.

Her claim had lost all meaning.

"Answer me," his mother insisted in her boardroom tone, attempting to scoot up in her bed, but wincing and staying put instead.

Will shook his head but wasn't sure if he meant that he hadn't fancied himself in love with Natalie once upon a time, or if he didn't want to answer her question, or if he just didn't like seeing his mother in pain.

"I'm not even sure I know what being in love is," he finally said.

"I thought Natalie loved me, but she left." He took a deep breath. He'd always been close to his mother but hearing the hurt in his voice embarrassed him. She was so strong. Would she think him weak for the way he'd so misread his relationship with Natalie? "She wouldn't have done that if she loved me. If what she claimed to feel disappeared so easily, then how could I ever trust in love?"

When his eyes lifted to his mother's he was surprised by what he saw there. Guilt.

Her painkillers must be an especially high dosage, because Rebecca Harroway Forrest was known for her steely resolve and emotional restraint. No way would she normally show what her expression gave away.

"She wasn't what I wanted for you," she confessed, moving her hand to pat his with her fingertips carefully to avoid triggering pain. "I wanted so much more and felt she stood in the way of you finding that something more. I was surprised she was the one to end your relationship, but I wasn't disappointed that she did."

He knew his mother had always held out hope that he and Stella would someday reunite, but had she purposely tried to push Natalie out of his life in her desire for it to happen? Whether his mother had intentionally conveyed her disapproval or had just failed to hide it, Natalie had known.

He faced the truth: he hadn't believed Natalie's insistence that his mother was trying to drive a wedge between them. He should have.

He should have done a lot of things.

Taking a deep breath, frustrated at her interference, he met his mother's gaze. "Then you should be happy because you got what you wanted."

Will had purposely not scheduled any procedures or appointments the following day so he could sit with his mother.

Other than getting up every so often to stretch his legs, he'd been beside her hospital bed for almost as long as she'd been in the private room, including having spent the night with his feet dangling off the end of a rollaway cot. No matter what she'd done, how could he not be there when the strongest woman he'd ever known wavered between dozing off and frustration at thinking her well-orchestrated world would fall apart if she had to take a health leave? Until a couple of months ago when his mother had confessed that she'd found a lump in her breast, Will had never seen a chink in her armor. His mother had been invincible. A powerhouse willing to take on anyone who got in her way. Which, unfortunately, apparently included Natalie.

Natalie. Had she worked late? Gone to dinner by herself? Started moving her belongings to her new apartment?

What had she wanted to talk to him about when she'd asked him to dinner last night? No one knew why he'd blocked his surgery schedule. Did she miss seeing him at the hospital today or was she grateful she didn't have to face him?

Will's father refused to stay away any longer and had arrived incognito that evening, saying he should be there when Dr. Shasteen talked to them about the pathology results.

When Dr. Shasteen knocked on the door, then came into the room, Will tried to read the man's expression and was glad he got right to the point.

"The surgery margins were good. We got all the cancer."

Will, his father and especially his mother let out a sigh of relief.

"What about the lymph nodes?" Will asked. "Were they clear?"

Dr. Shasteen smiled. "They were cancer-free and there's no evidence the cancer has spread anywhere else in the body."

"So, I can go back to work tomorrow?"

The doctor laughed. "It's barely been twenty-four hours, Rebecca. Keep icing your breast per the instructions I gave yesterday and give your body time to heal."

"I suppose I have no choice. Everyone at the company

thinks I'm away on business for the rest of the week," she mused. "I need to get back soon or that Jasper Wilson who's in charge while I'm away will be trying to convince the board that he should run my company. I'm positive he wants my job." Her gaze narrowed. "If the man wasn't such a brilliant businessman, I'd show him the door."

"If you ask me, you should let him take over more of your duties, so we have more free time."

Will winced at the look his mother gave his father.

"As if you're going to have any time after you win another term on the Senate," she accused.

He shrugged. "Maybe I won't win this term."

His mother looked horrified that he'd even consider not winning. Losing just wasn't in her nature. "Of course you're going to win."

"I'm just saying it wouldn't be the end of the world if I didn't and we took time to travel and see the world. This breast cancer thing has me rethinking life. We need to enjoy it more."

Dr. Shasteen cleared his throat, calling their attention back to him. "I know you're anxious to get back to work, Rebecca, but the earliest I'll consider discharging you is tomorrow. Then, at home, you're going to need to take it easy for a few days. I'd say to give it at least until Monday, then start back slow."

Will could see the wheels turning in his mother's head. Apparently, her doctor could, too.

"Slow means no more than eight hours a day that first week back. I want to recheck your surgery site prior to you returning full speed."

The doctor spoke for a few more minutes, answering his parents' questions and the few Will had. After Dr. Shasteen finished with his consult and left the hospital room, Will's father hugged his mother gently, kissing her and whispering things Will couldn't make out and didn't want to. They weren't an overly PDA kind of couple and Will found himself looking away at their private moment. He was superfluous, and perhaps even forgotten.

Relief hit as his phone pinged. Maybe it was the hospital saying there was a dire emergency and he was desperately needed, so he'd have a great reason to give his parents alone time.

If by any chance you finish with your plans, it's a lovely evening and I decided to go sit in the bleachers on Times Square to people-watch. There's a decent street band I think you'd enjoy.

Natalie. His pulse sped up, sending his blood rushing through his body, which probably explained why he felt a little light-headed at seeing her name pop up on his watch face.

He pulled out his phone and texted back.

Times Square? Alone?

Her message came back immediately.

Is anyone ever really alone in Times Square?

Staring at his phone, he smiled at her question. Or maybe it was the smiley face emoji that had his lips curving upward. Or the fact that his mother's pathology results had been good news. Or all of the above.

Realizing he was grinning at his phone, he glanced up, but neither of his parents were paying the slightest attention to him.

You're welcome to join me.

His heart thundered.

He glanced toward his hugged-up parents. Although he'd planned to stay with his mother again, that had been prior to his father's arrival. Based upon the satchel he'd been carrying, he planned to stay. Will definitely wasn't needed. Wondering if he was crazy, he made a quick decision.

"That was someone from the CVICU," he said, standing. True enough. Natalie did work in the CVICU these days, and right or wrong, he didn't want to tell his parents where he was headed. "Mother, I'm so glad your pathology results came back as well as they did." He kissed her cheek. "Sorry to run, but I've got to go."

Also the truth because he'd seen how they were looking at each other. Maybe his dad had been serious about not caring whether he won or lost his reelection. He supposed his mother's cancer had made them both look at life differently. Although, recalling his mother's urgency to get back to the office, perhaps not so much in her case.

Either way, he said, "I'll check on you in the morning." Then turning to his father, he added, "Make her take it easy."

To which William Sr. laughed, his hand affectionately caressing his wife's. "Me and what army?"

Will grinned and took off. Best he figured he had about a fifteen-to-twenty-minute walk to Times Square if he hurried.

Natalie sat on the second from the top bleacher, the only open space when she'd arrived at Times Square. She'd opted to take the subway rather than walk the entire distance from Callie's alone.

Will's comment about her being alone had her closing her eyes.

She'd not been sure if he'd even text back, but she'd been so restless all evening, wondering where he was, who he was with, missing him, that she'd given in to the temptation.

Callie and Brent had plans with friends. They'd tried to get her to go, but Natalie had wanted to give them time without her. On a whim, she'd decided to visit the busy heart of the city.

For as long as she could remember, she'd enjoyed people-watching. Times Square offered a diverse viewing, from locals trying to turn a buck to visitors from all around the world and from all different walks of life there for the sights.

A trio of street musicians had the crowd singing along as the usual assortment of costumed characters posed for photos for a fee. Sitting with her feet propped on the tiny open spot on the bleacher in front of her, Natalie listened to the music, but caught her gaze drawn to a grinning older couple who were holding hands and looking super cute, making Natalie wonder at their history. Had they spent their lives together, raised a family and now looked back proudly on what they'd achieved? A few rows down from her, a young family were just getting started on their life together. The mom and dad were close to her age but had three small children with them. The oldest looked to be about five and the youngest couldn't be more than a few months.

Soon, that would be her holding a little one. Her hand went to her abdomen as she'd caught herself doing more and more. A baby was there. Her appointment with her gynecologist might not be for another couple of days, but she'd had her positive home tests.

And in her heart she knew.

The moment Katrina had said the word *pregnancy* the truth had clicked in Natalie's mind. Maybe on some level she'd already known but had been in denial.

Will's baby grew inside her.

If her loving him hadn't won his heart, if her leaving hadn't spurred him into action, was there anything she could do to make him love her?

And fast.

Because Will was a good man, an honorable man. He'd want to do what was right by his child. Natalie wasn't sure if that would mean marrying her, but she suspected so.

If Will didn't love her before knowing about their baby, she'd say no to marriage. She wouldn't tie him to her if she didn't have his heart. Not anymore than her having his baby already would bind them.

She glanced down at the phone she held. Fifteen minutes had passed without another reply from Will. Where was he? Who was he with? The possibilities made her head spin. He had every right to be with anyone he wanted to be with, she reminded herself.

Natalie swallowed, then told herself she was going to put all this out of her head and try to enjoy the music and the happy tourists around her. Forcing a smile to her face, she began singing along with them as they kept tune with the band.

That's when she saw him. There, just crossing the street to step onto the concrete pad of Duffy Square, was the most beautiful man she'd ever seen.

She'd told him where she was, invited him to join her, and he'd come.

That had to mean something.

"Will?" She stood, waved her hands in the air. "Will,"

she called louder, hoping he could hear her although she supposed it was impossible over the band and their singing fans.

But Will had been scanning the crowd for her and smiled when he spotted her.

Smiled.

At her.

Melting her heart.

She smiled back, then gave a little wave as if to say hi. He made his way up the bleachers, excusing himself as he weaved around others enjoying the nightlife entertainment.

"You're right," he said as he squeezed onto the bench next to her. "No one is truly alone in Times Square."

Soaking up the warmth of his body next to hers, Natalie nodded. "True, but there are definitely some things enjoyed best when someone is by your side."

Rather than comment, he looked toward the street musicians who were now belting out a hit from the nineties and grinned, "You thought I'd enjoy this?"

She knew he would. He was a big sucker for eighties and nineties tunes.

"They're not bad for free," she quipped, wondering if he could see her pulse hammering at her throat.

"There is that."

And then with all the noise around them, silence fell between them.

Rather than force conversation, Natalie sat next to him, acutely aware of the way their bodies pressed against each other.

Parts of her that had felt dead woke up, apparently surprised and thrilled by his nearness. Was he as aware of her body as she was of his? He hadn't jerked away or made any comment about her having told him to not touch her. Ha, if only he knew how much she wanted his touch. If only he would— She paused. There was no rule that said she had to wait for him to make a move. If she wanted to touch Will, she could touch him. He might tell her not to or pull away. But if she wanted him, she was going to have to show him.

Not that the truth in her eyes wasn't shining brighter than the lit-up signs on the buildings around them.

Natalie reached for Will's hand and laced her fingers with his. His hand was warm against hers, even his signet ring. Warm, strong, capable of such great things.

At first, she kept her eyes trained on the band, refusing to look his way to judge his reaction. But when he still hadn't pulled away after close to a minute, she cut her gaze his way.

He no longer watched the band but stared at their entwined hands. His expression was torn and Natalie's heart hurt.

"I'm sorry I left my birthday party."

His gaze shot to hers. This wasn't going to be easy. But emotion surged within her, bubbling over to where she had to tell him, even if it left her vulnerable. She wanted to tell him so much, about the life they'd created, but she had to make things right between them first. If that was even possible.

"Every insecurity I'd ever had about us hit me full force at that party." She took a deep breath. "Your mother was so thrilled at Stella being there, so approving of her." She could do this. She could tell Will everything. She had to. "It wasn't that I wanted a gift, per se, but it was the fact that a pretentious party your mother put together that included your ex was my birthday surprise, and it set the tone for an evening that just kept getting worse."

"It wasn't."

Not quite sure she'd understood his low comment with the music blaring around them, Natalie asked, "What?"

"Your party was only the first part of your gift, Natalie. You left before we ever got to the next part."

"Oh." If only she could go back to that night, not leave in a weepy mess and instead show gumption in claiming Will as her own when he'd been on the dance floor with Stella. Taking another deep breath, she asked, "What was the next part?"

He shook his head. "It doesn't matter now."

It mattered to Natalie a great deal.

"If I had it to do over, I wouldn't have left. Not because of a gift," she rushed on, afraid he'd think that's what she meant, "but because it was wrong to leave the way I did."

His eyes dropped to their held hands, again. "If you could go back to that moment in time, what would you have done?"

"When I stepped out of the bathroom and saw you dancing with another woman? With Stella?" She thought for a moment, then said, "I'd tap you on the shoulder and ask you to dance with me."

His gaze lifted, holding hers. "What's stopping you?"

"Now, you mean?" Left a bit in shock by his question, she glanced around the concrete pad full of people. There were a lot milling around, watching the band, a few swayed a little to the music. "No one's dancing."

His eyes still focused on her, he shrugged. "That's a shame."

"Do you want to dance with me?"

"Are you asking me to dance, Natalie, or asking if I want to dance with you?"

Her breath caught. Will was here, was giving her the opportunity to ask him to dance. They'd be the only couple in each other's arms, but someone had to be first, right?

She stood, tugged on his hand. "I'm asking you to dance with me, Will, because I want to dance with you."

He hesitated and Natalie thought he was going to decline, that he'd set her up to shoot her down. She probably deserved him to publicly say no. Publicly because a few of the other benchwarmers had started paying attention to them.

"Why do you want to dance with me?"

"That's easy," she admitted. "Dancing gives me a reason to be in your arms."

His brow arched. "You want my arms around you? For me to touch you?"

More than he'd believe.

"Yes."

I want to touch you, to be so close I can breathe the scent of you in and feel your heartbeat next to my cheek.

She wanted him to hold her forever.

His gaze darkening, Will stood. "Okay, but let's hope the band plays something better to dance to."

Natalie had been so caught up in Will that she hadn't paid attention that the band now played a fast electric number. She wasn't a great dancer under the best of circumstances, but at the moment, she didn't care. Maybe the band would see them, take mercy and play something slow.

Hand in hand, they made their way off the bleachers to a vacant spot on the concrete. Despite the fast pulsating beat, arms around his neck, Natalie laid her cheek against Will's chest, imagining that she could hear his heartbeat over the thrumming of the city and the music. In her mind, his heart raced along with hers in a rhythm that was all their own.

Around them the city thronged, the song played and tourists snapped photos. Natalie didn't even care if they'd figured out who Will was. This moment was hers and she was lost in it. There was nowhere else she'd rather be than in his arms.

At some point the music slowed. Whether in Natalie's head or for real, she wasn't sure. It didn't make a difference. They swayed together and nothing else mattered.

This was where she belonged. With Will. Forever.

She looked up at him to tell him how she felt. But when she did, his mouth covered hers in a kiss.

A kiss of possession and anger and passion and hurt and so many things she wasn't sure how to label. Rather than try, she put her soul into kissing him back, not trying to hide the emotion filling her that she was once again experiencing his kiss.

When he lifted his head, Natalie stared at him. Knowing her heart shone in her eyes anyway, she whispered, "I love you, Will. I never stopped loving you."

Not something she'd intended to say, and something she shouldn't have said as Will reeled back, and at the same moment, the song ended.

People around them clapped, including the band.

Realizing they were being applauded, Natalie's cheeks heated, but she held Will's gaze. What she needed to see in those beautiful green depths wasn't there. No joy at her admission of love. No return of her feelings. Just shock. And uncertainty. And anger. And a whole lot of fight or flight.

Her knees wobbled.

"It's easy to get caught up in the chemistry between us, to momentarily forget the things that have happened and say things that in the light of day, you don't mean," he finally said, pulling away.

She started to answer, but before she could a commotion to their left caught their attention.

"Somebody help my husband!" a curly haired woman in her seventies cried as she bent over where a man lay on the concrete.

Oh! The sweet couple she'd been watching earlier.

Natalie and Will rushed over to where the man lay, not moving, his wife frantic as she shook him.

"Sir, can you hear me?" Natalie asked, dialing for emergency assistance as Will put his fingers to the man's brachioradialis to check for a pulse, then checked for breathing status.

"We were listening to the band, watching you two dance, then decided we'd join you for the next song. Only, he grabbed my hand, then collapsed," the woman said in a panicky voice, continuing to shake her husband. "Is he okay?"

Even as the woman was asking her question, Natalie's eyes sought Will's and he shook his head. No pulse and the man wasn't breathing.

"I'm a nurse," Natalie told the woman, keeping her phone held between her shoulder and her head, hoping her voice sounded calmer than she felt as she quickly pulled her mouth guard out from her small shoulder bag. "And this is Dr. Forrest," she said as Will placed his hands over the man's sternum, then Natalie identified herself, gave her location and requested an ambulance to the emergency worker who'd answered her call.

"Oh, God, no." the woman gasped as she realized they were initiating CPR. "He's going to be okay, isn't he?"

Natalie's heart went out to the woman, but she'd leave it to someone in the crowd to try to calm her. Placing her phone on speaker and setting it on the concrete, she bent to give the man two breaths in rhythm with Will's thirty chest compressions.

One. Two. Natalie breathed, then kept count with Will pressing hard into the man's chest with the base of his locked hands. And again, one breath, two.

Noises around Natalie faded as they attempted to save the man's life. Time seemed to have stopped as they worked, but Natalie supposed it was mere seconds before she felt the faint flicker of a pulse.

"Will!" she exclaimed, checking to see if the man was breathing on his own prior to giving an additional two breaths.

Nothing, but after delivering the second breath, she felt a small swoosh of air from the man's nostril. Then, he took a deep inhalation, seeming to gasp and cough at the same time.

Yes!

Natalie moved back a bit in case the man became sick to his stomach.

"Oh, John," the man's wife cried, taking his hand and giving in to more tears.

When his eyes opened, the crowd that had gathered around them clapped and cheered.

Although they'd revived him, Natalie knew the man was far from out of trouble. Something had caused his heart to stop, most likely an acute myocardial infarction.

Sirens blared, cutting into Natalie's haze. The ambulance arrived, and the paramedics joined Natalie and Will in caring for the man. Within minutes, they had medication administered, an intravenous line going and the man on a stretcher to load him in the back of the emergency vehicle.

"You'll see to it that she gets to the hospital?" Will asked, his gaze meeting Natalie's.

Not surprised that he intended to go with the ambulance, Natalie nodded.

And then Will was gone.

CHAPTER EIGHT

NATALIE'S STOMACH KNOTTED as she hesitated outside the ballroom. She'd spent most of the day at the glitzy hotel with Katrina and a crew of volunteers making sure everything was perfect for the charity event.

She'd been so busy working she'd not let herself think about the last time she'd been inside the beautiful ballroom.

So much about her life had changed since her birthday.

She'd not seen Will since their dance in Times Square the week before. When she'd arrived with Mrs. Jones at the emergency department, Will was already prepping to go into surgery with her husband to stent a couple of blocked arteries. She'd hoped he'd call or text her to let her know how the man was, but she'd not heard from him. Nor had she seen him at the hospital, because Connie had returned to work and Natalie was back in the ICU.

During a rare break, she'd gone to the CVICU under the pretense of bringing Callie a drink after her friend texted her that she was thirsty, and oh, by the way, a certain doctor was making rounds. Unfortunately, by the time she got her patients covered, clocked out and arrived, Will had come and gone.

In the meantime, she'd seen her specialist, had her pregnancy confirmed and had an ultrasound scheduled for the following Monday. An ultrasound she desperately wanted Will at.

Had she not known she'd see him at the gala, she'd have messaged or called to see him prior to her test because he deserved to be there, to see their precious baby with her for the first time.

Which meant she had to tell him.

Would tonight be her last chance to see him before having to tell him? Her last hope of having him admit that what he felt for her was more than chemistry?

She'd told him she loved him, and yet again, he'd not expressed the sentiment back. Her heart twisted as she recalled his words. How could he think she hadn't meant her proclamation of love? If only he could see what was in her heart.

Had his comment meant that she was caught up in their chemistry or that he thought anything he felt for her was only due to physical attraction?

"A lot has changed since the last time we were here."

"Oh!" She jumped at Will's voice echoing her earlier thoughts. She hadn't heard him walk up next to her. "I was just thinking that."

"Any regrets?"

Why was he asking? She'd admitted to her regrets when they'd been in Times Square. Was he wanting to rub her face into her mistakes?

"You know I do." Forcing a smile, tight though it was, she asked, "Doesn't everyone have regrets, though?"

"I suppose."

"I heard Mr. Jones got to go home yesterday."

His gaze studying her, he nodded. "He's doing well."

Reaching up to touch his arm, she teased. "He's a lucky man that New York's finest cardiac surgeon was within feet of him when he had his heart attack."

"That's an exaggeration but I'd say the same regarding your nursing skills. I appreciate you seeing his wife to the hospital. She's a sweet lady, but I'm not sure she'd have done well traversing the city on her own."

"No. They were visiting from Missouri. It was their first time to visit the city."

"That's what they told me."

"Too bad I was no longer in CVICU. I'd have enjoyed taking care of them."

"You weren't glad to get back to ICU?"

Natalie bit into her lower lip. Here was her chance to let him know how she was feeling. "I enjoyed CVICU well enough. It was great to work with Carrie, but, mostly, I miss seeing you, Will."

His gaze softened and she felt her hope rising. He cared. She knew he did.

"Natalie—"

"Heavens, this place is hopping."

Natalie winced as Will's mother and Stella stepped out of the ladies' room. The young woman's blond hair was piled up on her head with tendrils dancing about her face and her lips shined with a fresh coat of candy apple red. She was stunning to say the least.

Natalie sucked in a breath and held it, hoping the oxygen dissipated the dizziness that hit at the realization that Will had arrived with Stella.

Yes, a lot had changed over the past two months.

"It's not what you're thinking."

Swallowing the lump in her throat, Natalie nodded. "Okay."

If he said it wasn't, she'd believe him. Only, her throat felt so tight that breathing was difficult.

"Stella's date for the evening ended up being called

out of the city last minute, and so Mother invited her to join us tonight."

Natalie glanced toward Rebecca, meeting the woman's shrewd green eyes and refusing to look away. She nodded, acknowledging the woman. Although perfectly made-up, something was different about Will's mother. Perhaps just that she'd lost a few pounds.

What would Rebecca say to Natalie being pregnant? It wouldn't be good.

But Natalie wouldn't let the woman rob her joy in the fact Will's baby grew inside of her. She just wouldn't. So, she focused on the fact that this dynamite petite woman was her baby's grandmother, and she pasted a smile on her face. "Hello, Rebecca."

Rebecca's gave a quick nod her way, then replied, "Natalie."

At her name, Stella's eyes met hers in the way that happens when two women who are in love with the same man come face-to-face for the first time.

"I'm Stella Von Bosche," she said, holding out her slim hand. "Cute dress."

Trying to decide if the upscale fashion designer was being facetious, Natalie gave a tight, polite smile. "Thank you. It's borrowed from a friend," she said proudly, grateful Callie wore the same size and had the blue number from a Christmas party the previous year. Funny how time changed things. Once upon a time she'd cringed at the thought of wearing someone else's clothes ever again. "I'm Natalie Gifford."

"Nice to meet you," the woman said, smiling in a friendly enough way that made Natalie momentarily question if the woman truly was in love with Will or if Natalie had imagined that earlier look.

What was she thinking? Of course the woman was in

love with Will. How could any sane woman who knew him not be head-over-heels in love with him?

"I appreciate your generous donations for the Children's Cancer Charity, and I know the families benefitting do. As you probably know, you'll have the opportunity to meet several of them tonight." Natalie gestured toward the front of the ballroom. "The table reserved for the Harroway Foundation and its guests is in the front just to the right of the stage."

Her gaze went back to Will's, hoping that he'd suggest they meet up later, something, anything, but the soft look that had been in his gaze earlier was gone, replaced by a stern expression as he eyed his mother and Stella.

Not sure what to think, Natalie eyed the group of guests coming into the room. Katrina was with them and pointing her way. "Now, if you'll excuse me, I'm sure Katrina has a lot of last-minute things she needs me to assist with," she murmured, planning to go help her cochair. But before stepping away, she met Will's gaze. "Talk with you later?"

Surprise lit in his eyes and, after a moment, he nodded.

Natalie's whole body felt lighter as she walked away.

She sat with several of the families being represented by the charity including two of the mothers, who served on the committee. Although she only picked at it, the meal was delicious. Everyone at her table was friendly and her nausea stayed at bay. If she could have kept her attention and off the neighboring table where Will sat, she might have followed her table's conversation better, though.

Will sat by his mother and, if anything, was even more doting than normal.

A quick auction was held for high-end donated items, a short keynote took place, then the dance floor was cleared.

Natalie made small talk with one of the parents, listening at all they'd been through with their son's non-Hodgkin's Lymphoma diagnosis the year before. Listening to their story helped keep things in perspective.

No matter what, the most important thing was that her and Will's baby was healthy.

Will's mother let out a long sigh, causing him to turn in his seat toward her.

"Everything okay?"

"No."

Concern filled him. She was less than two weeks out from her mastectomy. He'd tried to convince her to stay home, but as usual she'd done what she wanted. "You're in pain? Do we need to leave? I can go get Dad from where he's talking with the governor."

His mother's perfectly shaped brows drew together. "Don't do that. He'll start trying to drag me home, and I've been cooped inside those four walls long enough. Besides, I'm fine."

So, she kept saying. But, regardless of how subtle, Will could see the toll of her surgery on her face and in how she carried herself.

"It's you I'm worried about."

Will's gaze cut to his mother's. "Me?"

"You've not heard a word Stella and I have said for the past ten minutes, maybe longer."

He'd have sworn he'd responded at all the appropriate times, but there was no denying that he was distracted.

Even now he fought to keep from looking toward his distraction.

"She looks beautiful tonight, doesn't she?" his mother asked. He started to ask who, but her brow hiked up. "Don't you dare ask me to whom I'm referring."

"Okay, I won't. And, yes, she does. She always does."

"Which has me questioning a few things."

"Such as?"

"Why you are here rather than over at her table."

"Because you need me," he instantly replied.

His mother burst out laughing as much as someone who considered herself a true lady burst out. "Although the sentiment is appreciated," she patted his cheek, "it's quite unnecessary. I'm fine and if I need something, I have Stella."

Stella, who had been chatting with the couple to the opposite side of her, turned, smiled at them and answered, "Absolutely. You don't have to stick around here, Will. I'll stay with Rebecca."

His mother shook her head. "Listen to you two acting as if I need someone to babysit me. Both of you go, dance, be merry."

Will's gaze narrowed at her suggestion.

"Oh," his mother assured. "I didn't mean with each other. I know you aren't in love with each other."

Stella's cheeks flamed.

"You're not, are you?" Will asked.

Stella shook her head. "I love your family, Will, and you as a person, but no, I'm not in love with you." She cut her gaze to his mother. "Sorry, Rebecca. I know it's what you wanted."

"It was," his mother admitted, but kept her gaze averted from his. Shaking his head, he suspected that, even hearing that Stella and he were not interested in one another, his mother wouldn't give up on matchmaking if she thought there was any hope.

There wasn't.

Will's gaze went beyond his mother to where Natalie

chatted with a family. She smiled, brushed a stray hair back from her face, then laughed at something said.

He would never feel anything more for Stella because of the woman he watched.

She'd told him she loved him again, shocking him as he'd been telling himself for weeks that she didn't—couldn't—have really loved him. His defenses had gone up, trying to protect his heart from further disappointment, but had Mr. Jones not had his heart attack when he had, Will suspected he'd have made a confession. One that was long overdue and that had been on his mind almost constantly since that night, since seeing the Joneses together, his parents together, and realizing he did know what love was. What true love was.

He'd known for months, but hadn't given the emotion a label, possibly because of the tension between Natalie and his mother.

That tension shouldn't have kept him from admitting the truth, from saying the words and showing Natalie how much he cared about her.

"We don't always get what we want," he mused, eyeing his mother as a crazy idea hit him. "But maybe, sometimes, we can have a second chance to make things right." Hoping he wasn't making the biggest miscalculation of his life, Will stood, held his hand out to Stella. "Would you do me a favor and dance with me?"

"Will, I think you're making a mistake," his mother began, but he shook his head, ignoring her.

"Your mother is right, Will. I'm not in love with you."

"Which is wonderful, because I'm not in love with you, either," he said, "but I do need you to dance with me. It's important."

Because he and Natalie needed a do-over and, hopefully, this time they'd both get it right.

Curiosity lit her eyes. "Then, yes, let's dance, and you can explain to me why our dancing is important. Because I agree with Rebecca and think you're making a mistake since I'm not the person you want to be dancing with. You should be asking her, instead."

Natalie excused herself from the young family she'd been talking with at a buffet table and turned to see where she was most needed to help.

Her gaze lit on a beautiful couple on the dance floor and her world shifted.

Will and Stella were dancing. He'd said she was there with his mother. Had Rebecca pushed them into dancing again?

Oh, good grief. This was torture. She didn't want to watch them dance.

What she wanted to do was tap Will on the shoulder and ask to dance. What would he do if she did?

Don't be stupid, Natalie. You told him you loved him. He knows how you feel. Nothing has changed. So what if you interrupt and he dances with you?

Everything. That's what.

Body shaking on the inside if not the out, Natalie steeled herself for whatever happened because, before the song ended, she would be tapping on Will's shoulder.

Unfortunately, what she should have been preparing herself for was coming face-to-face with Rebecca Harroway Forrest.

"Natalie," the woman greeted, eyes so similar to Will's pinning her in place.

Natalie sighed. This was way too reminiscent of her birthday party where Will and Stella had danced and Rebecca had filled Natalie's head with doubts. Even if she was Will's mother, Natalie wouldn't let the woman do that. Not ever again. She loved Will, wanted peace with Rebecca, but she wouldn't let the woman emotionally abuse her.

"Hello, Rebecca. If you'll excuse me."

Rebecca ignored her, then gestured toward the dance floor. "They're a beautiful couple, aren't they?"

Ice picks jabbed into Natalie's heart, but she held the woman's gaze. "Have a good evening, Rebecca."

With that she lifted her head, kept her shoulders up and stepped away.

"He doesn't love her," came from behind her.

Natalie paused, closed her eyes, then told herself not to do it, not to take Rebecca's bait. Nothing the woman had to say to her could end well.

Just keep walking. You'll be glad you did, she told herself. Only her feet weren't moving.

"What Will does is no longer my business." Although, perhaps, in some ways, with the baby growing inside of her, that wasn't completely true.

Rebecca had the audacity to laugh. "That doesn't stop you from loving my son, though, does it?"

Natalie cringed, then turned toward the woman she'd let get under her skin too many times, the woman whose approval she'd craved but never had. "You're right. It doesn't."

But having to put up with the likes of you is enough to make me want to have a drink, she added in her head.

Not that she would. Not with the baby growing inside her.

The baby who was this woman's grandchild.

She needed to be nice, but Lord help her, she wanted to tell Rebecca to go fly a kite.

"I was wrong about you."

Not knowing where Will's mother was going with her comment, Natalie held her tongue and waited.

"I didn't think you were strong enough to hold my son's attention, but you did." Rebecca's gaze shifted toward where Will and Stella danced and she sighed. "Love is blind that way."

"No worries, Rebecca. Will doesn't love me," Natalie automatically countered, then wished she hadn't. Not that it mattered. Rebecca surely didn't believe he did.

But the woman's gaze moved back to her and studied her, then she shrugged. "That's not my place to say. But if I were you and there was any chance that a man as wonderful as my son loved me, I sure wouldn't just watch while he danced with another woman. I'd do something about it."

Natalie gawked at Will's mother. Was she encouraging her to interrupt the dance? Surely not. Rebecca wanted Natalie out of his life.

"What is it you'd do?" she heard herself ask even though she suspected she'd regret it.

Rebecca's expression bordered on *Duh*... "Tell him I love him, for starters."

"I've done that," she confessed, not quite believing she was having this conversation.

"And?"

"He pretended to be asleep the first time and the second—" Natalie winced. Why was she admitting these things?

"Go on."

"He told me he could never trust me not to leave again."

Rebecca's lips thinned, then she nodded. "Trust doesn't come easily when you're a Harroway or a Forrest. When you're both…" She gave a knowing look.

"Will's had a lot of women attempt to take advantage of him in the past. Although he'd never admit it, probably not even to himself, that was a big part of his attraction to Stella. As my goddaughter, she was safe—or so he thought until she left. Until recently, I didn't understand why she'd done that, but Will was never in love with her and for her to get over him she had to put distance between them. Lovely girl, so I'm glad she's found success and happiness with her business."

Was his mother suggesting Natalie needed to go far away to get over Will, too? That that would make her successful and happy? There was no distance far enough to get her over loving Will.

Will would never be out of her life. Never out of her heart. And not just because of the baby growing inside of her.

Natalie faced Rebecca. "Why are you doing this?"

"Because you were about to leave."

Confused, Natalie shook her head. "I'm not leaving. I'm the gala committee cochair. I'll be here until the very end. Besides, what do you care if I leave?"

"I love my son."

"I love him, too."

"I know."

Stunned that Rebecca's voice sounded approving rather than condescending, Natalie blinked.

"You do?"

Rebecca nodded, her gaze going to where Will danced with Stella. "He's easy to love but doesn't always make the wisest of choices."

Meaning Rebecca didn't want him dancing with Stella? Was this some type of trick? Some mind game to get inside Natalie's head yet again?

"For months I wanted your approval, would have done

anything to have you invite me to lunch or show even the slightest support of my relationship with Will. You never did." She eyed Will's mother suspiciously. "Why now?"

Had she somehow learned of Natalie's pregnancy?

Heart racing, she waited.

"Because I've been paying close attention to my son since you left him. Just this evening, I've caught him watching you a dozen times." Rebecca laughed. "But only when you're busy and he thinks no one is noticing."

Will had been watching her?

"I've monopolized my son's time the past few months. There were things going on that I won't bore you with, but that we can talk about one day over that lunch you mentioned. But I realize that in distracting him with my personal issues, and my beliefs in what was right and wrong for him, that I interfered in his life beyond what I should have." She gave a little shrug. "I'd always thought Stella would be his wife someday and was determined to see Will properly settled, just in case things didn't go well."

Although not fully understanding what Rebecca meant, Natalie just waited for her to continue. She was too shocked to find words, anyway.

"But what I thought really doesn't matter. What Will thinks and feels is what counts." Rebecca took a deep breath, then reached over and squeezed Natalie's hand reassuringly. "As I said, I want my son happy."

Eyeing Will and Stella on the dance floor and realizing she was rapidly running out of song to interrupt their dance, Natalie said, "I want him happy, too."

"Then do something about it."

Will skimmed the gala guests until he spotted a certain redhead.

When he did, and realized who she was with, he

missed his step, smashing Stella's toe and causing her to stumble.

"Ow!" she complained.

"Sorry," he apologized, steadying her, his gaze not leaving the two women across the ballroom, deep in conversation.

What was his mother doing? Natalie had told him given the chance to redo the events that had taken place at her birthday party, she'd have interrupted his dance with Stella. He was giving her that opportunity, offering that chance for them to start over.

Only, this time they'd do things right.

But his mother wasn't supposed to be interfering.

Turning to see what had distracted him, Stella asked, "Don't you wish you were a fly on the wall for that conversation?"

Yeah, Will did and considered charging over to find out, then stopped himself. Maybe it was more than just Natalie and him who needed a redo. Perhaps his mother needed the chance to make things right, as well.

"You think Rebecca is giving her hell for having left you? Or ordering her over here?"

"I trust her," he assured, his gaze briefly flickering Stella's way and hoping his trust wasn't misplaced. If she believed him wrong, would she think it her God-given right to intervene a second time?

Stella gestured toward Natalie. "If you'd ever looked at me the way you look at her, I wouldn't have left." She gave him a pouty smile. "You're such a great guy, I'd have ended up married to you and not even realized I'd settled."

Will frowned. "I'm not sure if you just complimented or insulted me."

"A compliment. Every woman deserves a man to look

at her the way you look at Natalie. Anything less is set-
tling. You and I don't love each other so it would never
have been that way between us."

What could he say? He'd never wanted Stella the way
he wanted Natalie.

"The way I look at her didn't matter in the long run.
She still left." For which he carried a great deal of blame.
How could he have been so blind? So selfish for so long?
"I plan to win her back."

Stella's brow arched. "Which is why you asked me
to dance?"

"It's hard to explain, and I'm sorry to use you this
way, but Natalie and I needed a redo of my last dance
with you."

If this failed, he'd figure something out to let her know
what a fool he'd been. Some other way to give them a
chance to move on from the mistakes they'd both made.

"I'm still not sure I agree, but I hope it works out for
you."

"Me, too." God, he hoped he wasn't wrong.

Her eyes full of approval, Stella smiled. "Well, it looks
as if you're about to find out. She's on her way over here."

Natalie could do this. She could march up to Will, tap
him on the shoulder and ask to cut into their dance. She
didn't exactly have Rebecca's stamp of approval, but
Will's mother didn't seem to disapprove. At least, Natalie thought that's what their conversation was about.

Even if she did, Natalie would be doing this. This
dance, this moment, was her opportunity to correct the
mistake she'd made on her birthday. She wouldn't be
leaving tonight.

His back was to her when she reached him. Pulse
pounding in her ears, she tapped his shoulder.

When he turned and her gaze met his vivid green one, she sucked in a deep breath and went for broke. "May I cut in?"

He didn't look surprised to see her or by her question, just stared at her a moment.

When he hesitated, Stella leaned over and hugged him, whispering, "Pride is nothing to a lonely heart. Don't forget that and good luck."

Natalie's knees wobbled a little at overhearing the woman's comment. Was Stella making a play for him?

Natalie had made so many mistakes in their relationship. She knew that. No doubt, if he gave her another chance, she'd make many more. But she'd love him through them all.

Invisible hands grasped her throat as the blonde kissed Will's cheek, then smiled at Natalie and stepped away.

When Natalie just stood staring at him, he cleared his throat. "You wanted to dance?"

She wanted him.

Nodding and still shaky, she moved into his arms just as the song ended and another began. As they slowly began to sway to the music, she laid her cheek against his chest. This was where she belonged. In Will's arms, listening to his heartbeat, breathing in his scent and marveling at how every fiber of her being yearned for him.

She needed to tell him everything in her heart but savored moving silently in his arms for a bit longer. She could feel his inner tension, his inner turmoil.

She knew he cared for her, but he obviously also cared for Stella. Natalie had already poured her heart out to him and he'd walked away. What did she really expect to be different tonight? If he was happy she was there, he wouldn't be so tense at their dance.

The song ended much too soon. Natalie didn't step

away from him, just held her breath and stayed close as the next melody began.

She didn't want this moment to ever end as she might never be in his arms again.

Only she knew the new song would soon finish, that she needed to use these precious seconds to convince him that they deserved a second chance, and a third, and a fourth, if that's what it took. What they had was rare and precious and deserved to be cherished. She'd poured her heart out in Times Square, but she'd do so again and again and again as long as there was hope.

She leaned her head back to stare up at him, searching for words to tell him that she regretted everything that led to their breakup.

Before she spoke, he lowered his forehead to hers. "I thought I had this clear in my head, what I'd say to you if you asked me to dance, but I've been trying to figure out what to say from the moment you tapped on my shoulder, Natalie."

Natalie gulped. "Tell me I haven't lost you forever," she suggested. Would he be able to forgive her? Could he ever understand her reasons?

"You never lost me, Natalie."

"It's felt that way, and it hurts because I never stopped wanting you." She took a deep breath. "But I also want your attention and to be a complete part of your life and for you to let the world know that I matter. It's what I always wanted. It was wrong to leave, but I wasn't wrong to want those things."

Will stared down at the woman in his arms. The woman who drove him crazy. Because he was crazy about her.

This wasn't easy for him, but then, he suspected it wasn't for her, either. And yet, she'd risked his turning her away, publicly, when he'd already done so once. "The world didn't matter, Natalie. Just you did. I'm sorry I made you feel left out." Will brushed his fingers along the side of her face. "I knew you felt uncomfortable, and was trying to protect you from that, Natalie. I'm sorry I didn't make sure you realized that."

At his words, a tear trickled down her cheek.

"My sweet Natalie, I was such a fool to not cherish every moment with you. I should have shown you how much you meant to me every single day that you were in my life."

Natalie inhaled sharply, but quickly came to his defense. "It's not all your fault. I didn't feel as if I was good enough to be in your life, Will."

"You were. You are." Here went everything. Will took her hands into his, raised her fingertips to his lips and pressed a kiss there. "Part of me regrets the past couple of months more than anything, but another is grateful they happened."

"Grateful?"

"We both had issues, Natalie. Things we needed to work through. It took you leaving to open my eyes." To make him realize what was so very obvious. "There's something I should have done a long time ago," he continued. "Something I need to make right."

Then, Will cupped her beautiful face and stared into her big brown eyes. Everything he needed to know shined there. How could he have ever risked losing her?

"I love you, Natalie. I have from the beginning and never stopped. I never will. Forgive me."

Natalie's knees had been wobbly for some time, but now they were water. Her entire body was water and her eyes had sprung leaks.

Never had she heard more beautiful words.

"I should have told you long ago. Maybe I was in denial about how much I needed you." He wiped away a tear running down her face.

"I love you, too. You know I do."

He wiped another tear. "I thought so right up until the moment you left me and nothing has been the same since."

Would he ever be able to forgive her? To understand how crazy her emotions had been? That had she not been so hormonal, she might never have left? "I'm sorry, Will. I let my self-doubt ruin what was between us. I should have told you how I felt instead of pretending everything was okay for so long."

"You should have felt as if you could tell me, but at the time, I'm not sure I would have heard you if you had," he admitted, knowing that soon he'd tell her all about what his mother had been through. Maybe it would help Natalie to forgive her. "I should have made you feel so loved that you didn't feel like you needed to pretend to be okay. I'm sorry I didn't, Natalie."

"How could you make me feel loved when I doubted myself so much?"

"I should have tried." He slipped his Harroway signet ring off his finger. "I don't want you to ever question how I feel about you or how important you are to me. Not ever again. And I don't ever want you to leave me again, even if I deserve it."

Oh. My. Goodness. Natalie couldn't believe what he was saying, what he was doing. Had she fallen and bumped her head and was dreaming?

She must be because what Will did next couldn't be happening.

He took her hand into his and dropped to one knee.

"Forgive me and marry me, Natalie. Be my wife, the mother of my children, grow old by my side and never leave me, because what we have deserves a second chance and I won't get it wrong this time."

Legs giving out completely, Natalie dropped to her knees and leaned into Will. "Yes."

"Yes? You'll marry me?"

Had he doubted her?

"Yes!" she repeated. "Oh, yes. To all of it. Your wife, growing old at your side, being the mother of your children."

Around them, having noticed Will on his knee, guests cheered and clapped, including his mother and father, but Natalie barely noticed as Will lifted her hand to slide his signet ring onto her left fourth finger.

"We'll replace this with whatever you want," he promised, clutching where the too big ring fit loosely over her finger as he stood and helped her to her feet. "Maybe my grandmother's sapphire. I'd meant to give you the matching earrings for your birthday."

But she'd left before he had.

"I don't need jewels. Just you," she whispered. She hugged him, then pulling back, looked up into his eyes, and wondered how he was going to take what she had to tell him. "Will, there's something else I need to tell you."

"Anything."

"Part of the reason I've been so emotional over the past couple of months is because of hormone fluctuations."

"Hormones?" he asked, not following what she meant, then his brows lifted as he realized. "Seriously? You are?"

She nodded. "I saw my obstetrician this past week and she confirmed it."

"Oh, Natalie." He wrapped his arms around her and lifted her off her feet.

"I take it you're happy?" she asked, laughing as he spun her, then dropped a kiss on her forehead.

"As long as I have you. Never leave me, Natalie. I'm lost without you."

"Never," she promised, and she never did.

EPILOGUE

THE CITY'S TALL buildings became suburbs, then homes with big yards and gorgeous trees surrounded by acreage.

"Where are we going?" Natalie asked.

"It's a 'prise picnic, Mommy," three-year-old Willow reminded her from her safety seat in the back of the luxury SUV.

"You heard the boss," Will said, grinning as he kept his eyes trained on the road. "It's a surprise picnic so no more questions."

"Okay, sorry. No more questions." Wondering what her dynamic duo were up to, Natalie laughed and settled back into her seat to watch the vaguely familiar countryside pass.

Soon, they turned down a country road she recognized from where they'd been touring homes. She'd scoured the online virtual tours and they'd looked at several in person over the past few months. He'd taken a different route and she hadn't instantly recognized where they were until he'd made that last turn.

She opened her mouth, then clamped it shut when she remembered her husband, who was now singing along with Willow's song about bus wheels, would only remind her that she wasn't supposed to be asking questions.

She suddenly realized which house they'd toured was

located on this road. It was her favorite. She'd loved everything about the brick-and-siding house with its large front porch when they'd viewed it the previous month. She'd been disappointed when they'd learned it had sold earlier in the day. Will had made a significantly higher offer to the new buyers, but they hadn't been willing to let their find go. Natalie didn't blame them. She and Will looked at what felt like hundreds since, but none of them spoke to her the way the modernized farmhouse had, with its decent proximity to the train station to commute into the city.

"I recognize where we are."

"Do you?" he asked, still not taking his eyes off the road.

"Yes, we were here about six weeks ago."

"Hmm, maybe." But even as he said it the farmhouse came into view.

Natalie sighed. "It really is a gorgeous place. I wish the buyers had reconsidered your offer to buy out their contract. Has a similar home nearby come up for sale?"

"Not that I'm aware of. I wonder if the new owners are home?" he asked as he put his blinker on and turned into the driveway. "We could stop by and say hello, ask if they've changed their minds."

"Will!" Heart thumping, Natalie twisted in her seat to face him as he parked the car. "We can't bother them. I'm pretty sure your persistence in trying to change their minds semi-bordered on harassment as it is."

"We don't have to stay long. Just a quick hello. Besides, Willow needs some fresh air."

Giggles erupted from the back seat.

Rather than answer, Will came around and opened Natalie's door before freeing Willow from her car seat. He set their daughter on the concrete drive but held her hand. Immediately, she began squirming and dancing around.

Will and Natalie exchanged looks.

"Our princess needs a throne," he unnecessarily pointed out. "Sure hope someone is home."

Watching their daughter hop around, Natalie hoped so, too. The little girl had gone just prior to their leaving the apartment, but it was a long drive from the city.

They went to the front door, and Will rang the doorbell, but no one answered.

"It doesn't appear that anyone is here," Natalie mused.

"Willow isn't going to be able to hold it until we can make it back home." He reached for the door handle.

"Will!"

"What?" He grinned, feigning innocence. "Hey, it's unlocked."

"You're going to get us arrested," she warned.

He shook his head. "The owners will understand that a three-year-old couldn't hold it until she got back to the city."

"What if they have a dog? A big dog?"

He paused to listen. "I don't hear any barking."

Natalie didn't, either, but bit into her lower lip as Will opened the door, scooped Willow into his arms and stepped inside the house to head to the bathroom.

Should she stay on the porch in case the owners came home so she could try to explain?

"Mommy, I need you," Willow called.

Apparently she wouldn't be the lookout. Natalie stepped into the house.

"Surprise!"

Natalie's mouth fell open. To her left was a huge banner that read Happy Birthday.

In the dining room to the left of the entrance foyer,

her friends and family flanked a birthday themed table, complete with a large three-tiered cake. Her parents, her brothers and their families, Callie and Brent and their adorable two-year-old son, Will's father, and Rebecca, aka Grammy.

"My birthday isn't for another couple of weeks," Natalie pointed out, her gaze going back to her grinning husband.

"I didn't want you to wait that long for your present."

Realizing what he meant, what their being there meant, Natalie's eyes widened. "Really? The new owners agreed to sell?"

Looking quite pleased with himself, he nodded, reached into his pocket and pulled out a key with a ribbon tied around the opening. "I bought it fully furnished, but you're welcome to change out any of the furnishings to your taste. Happy birthday, honey."

"Oh, Will, it's perfect."

While Will took their daughter to the bathroom because she really did have to go apparently, Natalie hugged each one of their guests, saying how surprised she was and how wonderful it was that they were there.

"Will was right. This place suits you," Rebecca said, giving Natalie a kiss on her cheek. "Plus, it's got plenty of room to build a barn for Willow's pony."

"Willow has a pony?"

Rebecca smiled indulgently. "Will shouldn't have read her that horse story if he didn't want her to have a pony. It's all she's talked about since." At Natalie's wide eyes, she laughed. "Don't worry. I remember the rules on spoiling my granddaughter. I'll wait until her birthday."

Natalie laughed. "Because it'll take that long for us to have a barn built?"

Rebecca shrugged. "There is that."

When Will returned, Rebecca reached for Willow. "Come on, darling. Let's go outdoors with Grampy and see where we're going to have your playhouse built. For Christmas," she called over her shoulder.

Natalie and Will shook their heads.

"She has Mother wrapped around her finger."

"And she doesn't the rest of us?"

Will laughed. "You have a point. Now, come here so I can give you a birthday kiss."

Natalie wrapped her arms around him and kissed him.

"How did you know?" she whispered after their lips parted.

"That you loved this house and that I would move heaven and earth to give it to you?"

He would have, too. From the moment he'd professed his love at the charity gala, he'd set about showing her just how much every day since. She couldn't ask for a better husband or better father for Willow.

"That, but I meant that we needed more room for our family than we have at the apartment." She waited while her words registered, as his eyes widened, and his lips did the same.

"Really?"

She nodded.

He picked her up and spun her around, both of them laughing.

"This is your birthday party and I'm the one getting a gift. That doesn't seem fair."

"You can make it up to me later."

"Deal," he agreed, pressing his lips to hers again. "I love you, Natalie, and I always will."

Of that, and the fact she was always going to love him right back, she had no doubt.

* * * * *

LET'S TALK

Romance

For exclusive extracts, competitions
and special offers, find us online:

f facebook.com/millsandboon

◎ @millsandboonuk

▼ @millsandboon

Or get in touch on 0844 844 1351*

For all the latest titles coming soon,
visit millsandboon.co.uk/nextmonth

Want even more
ROMANCE?

Join our bookclub today!

'Mills & Boon books, the perfect way to escape for an hour or so.'

Miss W. Dyer

'Excellent service, promptly delivered and very good subscription choices.'

Miss A. Pearson

'You get fantastic special offers and the chance to get books before they hit the shops'

Mrs V. Hall